Yvonne Hughes was brought up in the Medway Towns, and still lives in Kent with her husband Gordon and two geriatric Golden Retrievers; the eldest of six children and beating her identical twin into the world by a mere twenty minutes.

Much of her working life has been in the financial sector; not bad for someone who was asked to leave the maths class to stop dragging the rest down to her dismal level. Despite this Yvonne gained a BA in Social Sciences with the Open University. Her two grown up children, Nichola and Jonathan, live in dread of being featured in her work!

www.yvonnehughes.co.uk

A TIME TO DIE

Yvonne Hughes

A TIME TO DIE

Vanguard Press

A CIP catalogue record for this title is
available from the British Library.

ISBN 978 1 84386351 9

*Vanguard Press is an imprint of
Pegasus Elliot MacKenzie Publishers Ltd.*
www.pegasuspublishers.com

First Published in 2007

**Vanguard Press
Sheraton House Castle Park
Cambridge England**

Printed & Bound in Great Britain

DEDICATION

To Gordon, Nichola and Jonathan;
you have my unconditional love.

ACKNOWLEDGEMENTS

BBC Radio Scotland's 'Write Here Right Now' initiative. Gordon, for your total support and for the web site. Writer Alex Mabon, for his encouragement and advice. Fellow dog walker, Carl, for background on the local prison. Google; brilliant research tool. Nic and Jon for their input. Ginny and Russell for their support and, most importantly, my identical twin sister Jackie Gingell for believing in me as a writer.

Prologue

A small pathetic piece of meat, no longer young and tender but he would taste it just the same. Hovering unsure in the corner, just like he always did, pathetic little worm.

It had been sometime since he had been aroused without doing it himself. It felt good, fucking brilliant. He hadn't felt like this in quite a while. His appetites had been suppressed. Like a special meal, you savoured the memory, longing for another taste. Now he was going to have it.

Never experienced the fear until it was too late, totally taken up with anticipated gratification. Dead before he had been satiated. This pathetic little worm had grown a backbone.

Chapter One

I would find them all, even if it took me to the end of my days and cost me everything I owned.

Mickey too had been looking, wanted to see if I had fared better than they had. He was too young to have experienced the horror. Our sister shielded him from it all. Made sure he got an education. He was the brains of the family, would be their salvation. Recounted the pain and degradation my sisters and brother had to endure. The family secret, that brought shame upon us all.

The abuse started a week after her first period. Frightened and confused with the changes to her body, too embarrassed to ask. The pain when he did it was so terrible, she felt sure she would die. She knew it was wrong, didn't think she would be able to live with the shame. A secret, no one must ever find out. He threatened to kill them all Mickey told me. The pathetic excuse for my father, told her to stop her whining, he himself had been taken when he was even younger. The little ones pretended not to hear, fearful that he might start on one of them.

The first baby he gave her she miscarried, wasn't even aware what it was, being only twelve. It would never have made it anyway, what with him being the father. The second child went full term but was stillborn. The social took it away; they said it wasn't quite right. Mum knew, cried and asked for forgiveness that she was unable to protect them. Said she was a useless mother. That was when the heavy drinking started.

Her third child, she was determined not to lose, or have taken away. He was still taking her but now she went to another place in her mind where he could not touch her soul. She had a boyfriend at the time, convinced herself that it was his. He didn't stay long though, cleared off when she told him she was late. Her baby would give her unconditional love and receive unconditional love and protection in return, especially protection. She had grown up very quickly the last few years, known more that she should.

Her baby was never alone with him. The abuse she endured would be nothing compared to the pain at finding out he was doing the same to her precious daughter. She never thought of him as Dad. Dads just didn't do that to their daughters.

Mickey told me all of this to help me understand. My brother John who I would never ever have the privilege of meeting. Mickey never met him either. Like me would never call him brother to his face but his story would be told to me just as it had been told to him.

John stepped off the platform just as the 5.45pm fast train from London came rushing through the station. It was his fourteenth birthday. Only when he had gone did they find the note he had left, realised that he had suffered too. John was sensitive, unable to take it anymore. He needed to warn them, wrote in his best hand writing, carefully keeping within the lines of the page. He thought he was the only one who had to bear the pain and shame.

I was the fortunate one. Elsie, our mother had fallen pregnant with me at thirteen years old. Her and Bill were not promised to each other until the age of sixteen, but even at thirteen years old he had appetites. The shame to the family was too much even by his standards and I was given up for adoption or rather sold to them, as my new parents told me when I was of an age to understand.

My beloved adoptive parents were killed in a head on collision. They left me a tidy sum, together with the business they had worked hard to build up. Their legal documents came to me, including my birth certificate. Now I had the legal and financial means to trace them.

I had employed a retired Chief Inspector to track them down. I thought him pompous. A few months into the enquiry, his guard began to slip. I saw the lonely gentle soul hidden within the aloof exterior. We were married by special licence before either of us could change our minds.

My Jacob died two weeks after his sixtieth birthday. Shortly before his death he became reconciled with his son who began staying with me to help nurse Jacob.

His son was a tortured soul, uncomfortable with his sexuality. Disowned by his mother, her religion more important than her own flesh and blood. After Jacob died, he asked if he could stay. He was so like my Jacob in looks and personality, it was as if I still had a part of him with me.

He became the son I had always wanted, even began calling me mum. We settled into a familiar routine. During the week, he stayed with me while he attended college. Weekends were his time to let his hair down, I never asked. It was none of my business, as long as he was happy.

My new-found sibling told me about the rest of the family. He didn't see that much of them but made sure they were provided for. They knew he had done well for himself but he was reluctant to let them know where he lived. They didn't push the matter. If they pried, he would stop sending the money they had come to rely on.

He had worked hard to drag himself out of a life he had no intention of going back to. They made contact with him by leaving messages on a mobile phone he had just for that purpose.

He advised caution in meeting them, apart from Mary. Mary he loved with a passion. Felt an enormous responsibility to care and protect her. She had been through so much already. She was beautiful with a childlike innocence about her.

Mary had been the result of a liaison between our mother and the Social Worker assigned to the family. Unfortunately, when she told him of the pregnancy, he was absolutely horrified.

His career was important to him, more important than her. Besides he already had a wife and children, why would he want to take on her lot?

She threatened to tell the authorities. The word of a traveller against that of a social worker, he would deny everything. She stood no chance. Even had to force herself to have painful degrading sex with the bastard William Smith, so he might think it was his.

But he found out. He was being laughed at and it was all her fault. The beatings came more often always to abort the baby, kicking her in the stomach when she fell to the floor. He didn't want the kids they already had, what made her think he wanted another one, a bastard at that. After one particularly bad beating when she struggled to function, she knew the next beating could be her last.

That's when she began to drug him with her pills. Combined with the alcohol he became a docile zombie. Elsie had thought to end his life. What stopped her were the children. The family would be split up, sent into care. She had already lost one child, had no idea where she was, if she was happy, well fed, and had a good life. She wasn't prepared to split the rest of them up. When she was gone, they would only have each other, need each other.

Mary had been born with red hair, the image of her social worker father. She was a sickly child and cried continuously. William Smith hated his bastard daughter, dared Elsie or the children to pick her up and comfort her. As a young child she was shown little affection but Jean, she would sneak her into her bed during the night, put her back before anyone realised.

Mary developed autism, found it difficult to make eye contact, slow in her development so the doctors said.

My mother Elsie died three months before I found Mickey. Mickey said it was of a broken heart; the Coroner had ruled suicide, her mind impaired by alcohol. They found her dead on the railway line, clutching an old black and white photograph of John.

Chapter Two

Spread-eagled, naked on the quarry-tiled floor, he took up much of the limited space. Dragged out to attempt resuscitation, it failed. Pads still attached to his chest, a portable oxygen cylinder and mask lying by his head, showing the amount of effort put in.

The body was still soft and pliant, getting colder by the minute. Eyes open staring in shock, damaged blood vessels clearly visible. Long thinning grey hair, plastered against his head, sparse chest and pubic hair, signs of an older man. The rough calloused hands placed downwards on the floor, the knuckles beginning to show signs of arthritis.

Detective Sergeant Jonathan Adams squatting beside the corpse stared at the knuckles, each one giving a choice of 'Love' or 'Hate'. There were other tattoos on the weathered body.

The policeman looked around the bathroom. A stained faded towelling dressing gown casually thrown over a red plastic chair, the belt soaking up water from the floor. Wash bag and towel balanced precariously on the edge of the washbasin. An electric razor dangled from the point above the mirror. He examined the lead for signs of an electric malfunction. The emergency cord untouched, out of reach. Shortened with the excess looped up in a knot. That was against regulations for a start.

"Bugger all chance of any decent forensics." Jonathan Adams grumbled as he took in the scene clicking away with his disposable camera. Scenes of Crime would take the official photographs. Twenty years and still he hadn't made it past detective sergeant. Not that he was too bothered, enjoyed his life at the sharp end, damned good at what he did. His attitude to authority he had been told held him back, needed to be more of a team player, able to carry out orders without question. Networking. Kissing backsides more like. The extra money would have come in useful though. With a bigger salary, he would have been able to do much better than Doreen.

Jake Mortimer, trainee Detective Constable, had been dragged from the canteen to go with Detective Sergeant Jonathan Adams. Jake had completed his five-week stint on the Detective Training Course at Hendon only recently and was surprised to be working in CID so soon. Thankful for the opportunity a bout of food poisoning, courtesy of the staff canteen had given him.

His uniform supervisor had marked his card. Jonathan Adams was a dinosaur. Even claimed he kept a silver whistle in his top pocket. However, he was also honest and dogged, the sort of bloke you would want by your side in any situation. That suited Jake. He could learn much from Adams, would make good use of the chance he had been given.

"They need it to be natural causes otherwise they might be found to be negligent. Reflects badly on them, so the Staff Nurse said." Adams looked up as Jake finished talking.

"Well they would hope for a natural, much more tidy that way. His time was nearly up anyway. Look at him, more wrinkles than your shirt and I don't mean from the bath. The broken veins around the nose got to be a heavy drinker. What was wrong with him anyway?"

Jake glanced down at the clipboard taken from the end of the old man's bed.

"His notes show he is, sorry, was sixty three years old. Still had a lot of living left. No indication why he was here, just the usual investigations; heart, lungs, blood."

"He looks to have done most of his living already. Does he have a name? The tattoo on his arm says Mum but I'm guessing he's not known by that." Adams laughed at his own little joke. Embarrassed by his omission, Jake fumbled with the paperwork.

"A Mr William Smith, semi-retired, Church Warden. The next of kin is down as a Frederick Smith, son."

"Freddie Smith, not 'the' Freddie Smith, otherwise we are in trouble?"

"Somebody you know sir?"

"If the drink was in Freddie, he could be quite vicious. Sober just a nasty piece of work. Still, common enough name, we may get lucky and it's not the Freddie Smith I know. I can't imagine Freddie Smith's old man being involved in the Church, unless it was to thieve the lead off the roof."

In his mind, Jake was running through the order of securing a scene of crime. The theory was one thing but when you were out there actually involved, well he was frankly excited and terrified.

After placing the clipboard back at the foot of the bed he turned his attention to the locker, taking great care not to leave prints. On the top he found the usual, plastic jug of stale water and a box of tissues. A cardboard dish was the receptacle for a dried out orange and an overripe banana. He had no latex gloves with him so used the end of his pen to poke around in the locker.

In the main compartment, he found a couple of lad's magazines, a box of Quality Street and tucked right at the back, hidden from view a small half empty bottle of whisky. The bottom compartment was empty, where his dressing gown and slippers would have been. He noted the items in his book, leaving them for Scenes of Crime.

Hanging over the metal headrest was the only card. A get-well message from his Church family. God would be looking out for him and they were all praying for a speedy recovery. Not hard enough it seemed. He checked under the bed but all he could see was dirt and dust.

The ward was on the second floor of the main hospital building. Jake knew it was important to have a sketch plan of the area.

Nelson Ward was set up as six bays off a wide central walkway. Each bay consisted of eight beds with side armchairs and standard hospital lockers. The windows were set up high affording no view for the patients and staff. A very large ward, with few staff, anybody could have wandered in.

Standing by the side of the bed, the nurses' station was not visible from the bay. On the opposite wall was a concave mirror to view the area. It too was very high up, hadn't been cleaned for quite a while.

There was a Fire Escape next to the bed. Jake thought it looked a promising means of entry, as the door was partially hidden by the privacy curtain when it was shoved up close to the back wall. He examined the door. It didn't appear to be alarmed and was not secured; had been pulled to, giving the appearance that it was closed. Jake made a note to ask when it was last checked.

He pushed open the door and went out on to the fire escape. The small landing was littered with cigarette ends. The metal stairs down were covered in bird droppings, slippery and quite dangerous. It looked to have been recently used, but there appeared to Jake no discernible shoe prints. There was a concrete path from the bottom of the fire escape around the building to the main car park. The designated meeting point in the event of an evacuation.

The sound of raised voices led him back inside.

*****

"We need this facility. The other one is out of action, a blocked drain. What are we expected to do?" Get it unblocked thought Jake. She scowled at the pair of them, barely disguising her anger and frustration. Adams put on his best grin and held out his hand.

"I'm in charge for the moment madam. Detective Sergeant Jonathan Adams, and this is trainee Detective Constable Jake Mortimer."

Both men held up warrant cards. Jake stood to one side, embarrassed. In the rush to catch up with DS Adams, he had left his warrant card in his locker. Hoped she would not notice that his was a railway warrant. Fortunately, he justified barely a glance.

Jonathan smiled, proffered his hand to the smartly dressed woman. She did not return the smile but attempted to wield her authority over the proceedings. The small ones are always the bossiest and cutest thought Jonathan Adams. He liked them feisty.

"Tamara Jones, Assistant Senior Hospital Administrator. You are stopping the staff from working, disrupting ward routine. There are sick people here."

"Sorry madam, it may be a suspicious death. It will take as long as is necessary."

"It's Ms actually." Jonathan Adams smiled, not taken yet then.

"I'm sure the victim is not too happy about it either. Probably mortified at inconveniencing you." Jonathan chuckled at his little joke, lost on Ms Jones.

"But the body has already been moved. Staff attempted resuscitation."

Jonathan Adams already knew this; he was still trying to figure out how he was going to explain it to his governor. Forensics would be a nightmare to sort out.

With a huff she turned on her heel and walked out of the bathroom, careful not to trip over the body or look at it directly.

"Nice legs, wonder if she's spoken for?" It never occurred to him that she would be out of his league. Jake doubted very much that he would have been able to pull a woman like that anyway.

As Ms Jones walked past the nurses' station a hand shot out to grab her arm.

"Tammy, do we get the bathroom back yet or what?"

"I think you'll find it is 'or what' at the moment Joyce. I need to report to the Boss. Just what I need, interrupting him on the golf course."

Joyce watched as Tammy continued on out of Nelson Ward. As the Staff Nurse in charge, they would try to lay the blame with her, because that's the way they operated. Well she wouldn't go down without a fight that's for sure.

Yesterday's Ward Report had not yet been collected, so she was able to slip in a footnote concerning her unease over staffing levels.

"Lisa, go and see if the plods would like a cup of tea,"

"Sure Staff, the young one is quite cute don't you think? I wonder if he's spoken for?"

She preferred her men a little on the rough side.

Adams was waiting on his Supervising Officer Bryan Low. Detective Inspector Bryan Low loathed front line policing, ensured he was never around when a shout went down. Bryan Low had political ambitions. Preferring the networking side of the business, he was out on one of his 'jollies', left the mundane to his Detective Sergeant. It irked Jonathan Adams that he usually ended up doing the work of a detective inspector but on a detective sergeant's salary. You could learn from Inspector Low his governor had told him. Learn how to skive, that's for sure.

"Sergeant, you have a 'phone call. Please take it in the office, not at the nurses' station." He had missed lunch and was beginning to feel the effects.

"Thanks nurse. Any biscuits to go with the tea then?" He winked and gave her his little boy lost look. She sighed. It might have worked had he been ten years younger but not now.

"It's Staff to you and I would appreciate you making it brief as we can't have that line tied up for long." Jonathan watched her bustling down the ward. He quite liked bossy women, had fantasies of being dominated by one in a leather cat suit wielding a whip. Mind you he liked most women, particularly if they put out for him. Now in his early forties, pulling was becoming more difficult. Nurses and policewomen in uniform did nothing for him, but out, well that was a different matter. Suitably chastened he mumbled, "Yes sorry. Jake, stay here until the Scenes turn up. See if you can salvage something from the mess." Jonathan followed Staff cursing the fact he was unable to use his mobile. He needed to find out if William Smith deceased was related to Freddie, needed access to HOLMES.

The voice at the other end of the 'phone compelled him to make rude gestures at it, becoming more angry and frustrated.

"Yes sir, as long as you give permission. But it's not usual prac... No sir, I'm not questioning your order it's just not the way this usually happens. It's just that he may be related to... Fine!"

Unbelievable! Walking back towards the bathroom, he found porters already waiting to move the body.

"Sir? They want to take the body, that's not right! Scenes of Crime haven't been over the place yet."

"Let them move the body. Defective Inspector Bryan Low, our finest, has given permission apparently. Fortunate he was playing golf with the Chief Executive of the Primary Care Trust. They were able to come to an agreement. They get their bathroom back and we get screwed."

Chapter Three

Even with the toughened glass they could all hear. Embarrassed, most pretended they couldn't. Not Detective Sergeant Jonathan Adams. About time too! He was beginning to think he was the only one who could see Bryan Low for the useless article he was.

"So tell me Bryan, did you even do basic training at Hendon?" boomed out the governor.

"Well actually." Bryan Low was doing his best to retain his composure; aware their voices could be heard outside.

"It's a rhetorical question Bryan. You should be grateful that Adams was first at the incident." Adam's habit of using a disposable camera, as a back up, had saved what little scene of crime had been left. Adams, going over his head was bad enough but to show him up as incompetent.

"Adams will be the Senior Investigating Officer on this case, reporting directly to me, do you understand?" Detective Chief Superintendent Arthur Fisher spoke to him as though he were a slow child.

"Yes sir, but SIO? I mean, he is only a sergeant after all."

"That Sergeant will have forgotten more about police work than you will ever know and still be a better copper. For a start, he would not have allowed the body to be moved before forensics had arrived on scene."

"But sir, the scene had already been compromised. In the interests of the smooth running of the hospital, I thought it prudent…" he was interrupted before he could finish his explanation.

"There may still have been some trace, now we'll never know. Anyway, you have been seconded out of my department."

"Where to sir?"

"To who ever I can find daft enough to take you, now get out before I really lose my good nature and start raising my voice!"

Jonathan beamed at Bryan Low as he passed his desk. Today was turning out better that he had hoped after all.

"Adams, it seems I'm to be seconded to a more urgent case. You will be running this investigation, under strict observation obviously."

"Sir."

"Fisher will not always be around to protect you. Watch your back."

"Yes sir, I understand the new electronic filing system needs your expertise."

"Adams get in here and bring that young plod with you."

Jonathan plonked himself down in the recently vacated seat. Jake stood to one side behind him, note pad ready.

"Inspector Low has been seconded to another department where his expertise is much required. Adams remove the smirk from your face! You will be running the investigation as Senior Investigation Officer but under my supervision. I will be taking a keen interest in the proceedings, including scrutinizing expenses, do we understand one another?" Both nodded.

"I also expect to have daily updates on my desk every morning."

Adams began to protest about the lack of an experienced officer as his number two.

"We're short handed, either you want this or not. I think Mortimer has the enthusiasm and intelligence to work even with you. He's completed his training I understand. Besides, he's all we've got at the moment. Any problems with that?"

"No Governor."

"Where are you up to so far?"

"The body was removed from the hospital half an hour ago and should be in the basement. I'm following a lead concerning the family member."

"Best get going then." Detective Chief Superintendent Arthur Fisher opened his filing cabinet and took out a thick file. This was the signal they had been dismissed.

The station took up the ground floor. The rest of the building was County Headquarters. The basement had become the county mortuary, recently updated with state of the art equipment and the latest computer technology. They took the stairs, Adams inhaling the stale nicotine wafting up. Six months he had given up and still he missed it.

Adams swiped his card at the main door. The smell of disinfectant and rotting vegetables greeted him. Cold, it was too cold for Adams' liking.

"Hope you're not going to faint on me."

"No sir."

"If you fall, make sure it's backwards. Attended one where a plod fell and landed on the corpse."

Jake had attended a post mortem as part of his training.

Last year, he identified the body of his father after a road traffic accident, his stepmother being too distraught to carry out the task. If he could cope looking at the mangled body of his father then viewing a dead stranger shouldn't be a problem.

The ever-cheerful Bert handed them plastic aprons and shower caps. He had been the mortuary attendant at Headquarters for as long as Adams had been on the force.

"Sorry Bert, no time to chat today. Has the Doc' started yet?"

"You'd better get your arses in there, he's not happy."

"You're supposed to be here when I start. I'm a busy person, my time is precious." James Macdonald glared at them blinking rapidly, always did when he was annoyed. The small scar under his right eye more prominent, bobbing like a rowboat on a stormy sea. Adams had asked him once how he had come by it. Seems he did fencing whilst at university. Posh persons' sport, he might have guessed. "Not that good at it then?" he had asked him after the admission.

James Macdonald viewed unpunctuality as an outrageous transgression, not to mention a slight on his profession.

"James, James, what can I can I say. I'm so so sorry.

You know these young plods, needed to build up his courage to come in."

Jake shot him a scathing look.

"Well now you are here, I can tell you it was no accident or natural causes. Mr Smith was murdered, drowned in fact."

"How do you know he didn't just slip or faint and go under?"

"Well young man, the marks around this throat and on his chest are a bit of a giveaway. It appears that someone climbed in the bath with him, knelt on his chest and held his head under. His penis was partly engorged at the time of death."

"Was it a self-induced 'stiffie'?" James Macdonald shook his head, didn't think it had been.

"But it's a single sex ward."

"Adams, intercourse has been known between men. He was in the throes of ecstasy, probably eyes closed, didn't see it coming."

Jake attempted to suppress an embarrassed giggle as Jonathan Adams blushed.

"That's not what I meant. He was ill. I should have thought that sex was the last thing on his mind."

"You will have my full report by tomorrow morning, but I can tell you that he had advanced lung cancer. Had no more than a few weeks left anyway."

"Thanks I'll look forward to reading the full text as and when."

As they walked back towards the exit, they discarded their hygienic coveralls.

"Sir, what I don't understand is why if he only had a few weeks left would anyone bother to murder him? Why take the risk?"

"How the hell would I know why?"

They walked back into the CID area. One of Jake's colleagues from Blue Watch was setting up the whiteboards. A television and video recorder had been put in the corner. The uniformed constable handed Jonathan Adams a printout from CRIS, the Crime Reporting Intelligence System.

"Jake we're going out. Isle of Sheppey. Freddie boy is on holiday down there at her Majesty's pleasure."

"That rules him out then sir?"

"At this stage, I rule nobody out."

"Shall I sign out a pool car sir?" Jake had no desire to use his pride and joy on police business.

"Well I'm not walking."

The Isle of Sheppey housed a large prison complex consisting of three separate prisons: Elmley, Swaleside and Stanford Hill. It should by his reckoning take a couple of hours to get there. Adams knew the way, spent part of his childhood on the island.

It would be usual for someone at the prison to notify an inmate of the death of a family member but Adams wanted to do it, see Freddie's face when he received the news.

Elmley was in part a Category C prison and shared a site with Swaleside and Stanford Hill on the Isle of Sheppey. The records show that Freddie had been banged up in Elmley for the past sixteen months. Jake parked the car under the trees after dropping Adams at the main entrance; apparently the twenty-yard walk to the reception was too far.

"What do you mean he's not here? He's still got three months, even with time off for good behaviour, though knowing Freddie there wouldn't be any?"

"Well sir, if you would listen, I will tell you. Fredrick Smith was transferred to a Category D open prison four days ago. I expect the system hasn't been amended at your end yet."

"Haven't any of you got brains, surely updating records should be the first priority?"

"Well if you care to walk across the main car park to Stanford, you will be able to interview him."

"Numpty," Adams muttered under his breath.

"Pillock," muttered the officer at the Gatehouse.

Freddie had changed very little. Heavier perhaps but still the same skinhead hair cut and gormless look about him.

30

"Freddie, you don't remember me do you?"

"Should I, you all look the same to me, pointed heads, big feet."

"Well I remember you. Filled out a bit, lost your good looks."

"Doesn't do to have good looks in here."

"We're here about your father Mr William Smith."

"What or who's the old bastard done this time?"

"He died early yesterday morning."

Freddie shrugged his shoulders.

"So? Do I get to go out for the funeral then?"

"When did you last have contact with him?"

"You really dim or what? I'm doing a two stretch. Don't get out much these days." He laughed at his own joke.

"Do I get compassionate or what?"

"That's not for us to decide. Aren't you curious as to how he died?"

"Dead is dead!"

"You know anyone who would bear a grudge against him?"

"You telling me it weren't natural?"

"There is a possibility his death may have been suspicious, so any help would be appreciated."

Freddie said nothing, began chewing his fingernails. He'd never been a grass in his life, was not about to start being one now.

"We'll be in touch."

Completing formalities, they handed in their visitors' badges and were escorted back to the main gate. All this way for five minutes, Jake was at a loss to understand Adams' logic.

"Sir, I was talking to one of the officers. Seems Stanford is a category D, Freddie could have absconded and then slipped back."

Heavy traffic meant is was after seven when they arrived back. They picked up their messages on the way through the main reception.

31

Uniform had located and interviewed more of William Smith's family. Freddie had a twin sister called Jean. She had been advised of her father's death, taken it well by all accounts. Said 'she would let the rest of the family know'.

Their youngest brother, well he had got too uppity to talk to them apparently. She had a mobile number and would try and make contact. They had not been made aware of the seriousness of his illness.

"Seems he had a number of visitors while he was on Nelson. His daughter and granddaughter mainly and a bloke one of the nurses seemed to think was the granddaughter's partner. He seemed to get on well with the old man."

Probably the one who brought in the alcohol for him, thought Jake.

Chapter Four

When Detective Chief Superintendent Arthur Fisher said he would be overseeing operations, Jonathan Adams didn't think he would be supervising this closely. Arthur Fisher had put his reputation on the line, arguing Jonathan Adams was good enough. Any damage to his career would be by his own hand, not that of Jonathan Adams.

"The interviews with the hospital staff. I don't appear to have them on my desk. First forty-eight hours are crucial to any investigation. You haven't forgotten?"

"No sir. We were only able to conduct preliminaries. The Staff Nurse in charge requested a Federation representative. Thinks the hospital will hang her out to dry. We've arranged to interview this afternoon. The hospital is making an office available."

"Better not keep you then."

"Well that's me well and truly dismissed," he mumbled walking back into the main office. No prospect of sex tonight. The boss expected full interview transcripts first thing in the morning.

"Tell me Jake how's your typing and social life?"

"Both fine I think sir."

"Well one out of two's not bad."

Adams had borrowed a marked car from traffic, save finding a parking spot at the hospital.

Ms Jones had made an office available, one of the small staff rooms, good job they didn't have a cat with them, thought Adams.

"Staff has her break in five minutes. I have arranged extra cover in case you take longer than ten. Her staff representative has been alerted and he will be sitting in with her."

"We would prefer to speak to Staff Nurse Lloyds without her union representative. Is he employed here?"

"Yes he's one of our porters."

"We don't have a problem if she requests legal representation, that is her right but as a porter, he may be involved."

"Well you had better tell her then. We're not really on speaking terms at the moment," sniffed Tammy Jones as she walked away.

Staff Nurse Joyce Lloyd was not happy.

"You know they want to fit me up for this. Covering their backsides in case his family sue. Negligence. Always comes down to the one in charge right?"

Not in our job thought Jonathan.

"Just need you to run through the events of Wednesday again."

"We did the usual, checking on the patients during the night. You can check the log if you want."

"Nothing out of the ordinary?" Staff Nurse Lloyd shook her head.

"We usually wake the patients around six, six thirty. We wake them early when the cleaners come in. If you're lucky, they sometimes give a hand."

"Did Mr Smith need assistance to go to the bathroom while he was here? I'm trying to establish if he was mobile."

"Notes do not state bed rest, so he would be expected to make his own way to the bathroom. He only came onto the ward on the Monday. Rude and racist to other members of staff, I had to warn him. He had one of our tea ladies in tears, called her a monkey, told her to go back where she came from."

"When did you realise there was a problem?"

"Another patient, needed to use the bathroom. I heard him shouting and banging on the door. I was doing rounds, checking that all clinical notes were up to date. I was the nearest, so I went over. Water was seeping under the door. I used the pass key and there he was."

"It was you who drained the bath?"

"As I tried to lift him, his foot caught the chain and released the plug. One of the porters was on the ward and he came and assisted me. I started CPR but could see it was too late, but you have to try anyway."

"This porter is he the one who's the union rep?"

"No. Look, you have my other statement; I've really got to go back on duty."

"I thought Ms Jones had arranged extra cover for you?"

"She has, but the cow's taking it off my lunch hour."

"We may need to speak to you again Miss Lloyd."

"I'll still be here, at least until the enquiry is finished, then I'll be emptying bed pans on the geriatric ward. Evenings after work are best for me. Perhaps I could meet your constable for a drink if you need to ask me any more questions."

Jake bent his head, furiously scribbling in his pad. He was already getting grief from his partner. If he was seen with a strange woman, it didn't bear thinking about.

Trainee nurse Lisa and the porter, Sid White confirmed what Joyce Lloyd had told them. The incident log had been signed by all three of them. Jake made a note to cross check his name for any previous.

"We need to find someone who saw him go into that bathroom."

"Well sir, I checked the interviews uniform did with the patients. Most were still asleep when it kicked off."

"Cleaners it is then. Have you got the list?"

"Agency Staff. We need to contact the company. They use a number of different agencies it gives them more flexibility. Ms Jones is yet to come back to us on which company."

"Staff Nurse Joyce Lloyd was holed up in her office, eating a doughnut. From the small office, the bay was unable to be seen. It would have been easy for somebody to sneak in."

"Don't look at me like that. I should know better but it's the sugar rush, I need it to keep going." She had mistaken his look of envy as one of admonishment.

"Cleaners, how many were on that morning?"

"Two, possibly three. Depends on what they are doing that day. Light or heavy clean."

"Are any of them on duty now?"

"Different shifts. The lot now are the afternoon shift. They work on early, mid and late."

"Can you at least confirm which agency was used on Wednesday?"

"Sorry, you need to speak to Tammy."

Jonathan made his way back to the Administration Office. Showing his warrant card, he requested the list of agency cleaners on duty on Wednesday.

"Well I'm not sure Tammy, Ms Jones, I need her permission, and she's not here."

"Ms Jones advised me it would be here for collection. Do I need to contact her Boss then to sort it out?" The thought of involving the Chief Executive sent her scurrying off, returning a few minutes later with the required information.

"I've listed them all, sometimes they swap wards when they arrive. A number of them can't speak English and prefer to work with their friends."

A list of two or three now increased to around twenty. Hopefully the Agency Manager would be able to narrow it down. He made a quick call.

The Primary Care Staff Agency was housed above Adi's Kebab Shop in the High Street. A narrow flight of stairs led directly into a reception area. A notice on the desk advised to ring the bell for attention. Jonathan left his finger on the bell.

"Alright, where's the bloody fire?"

She really didn't have the figure for a short denim skirt and as for her skimpy top… well he decided not to go there.

"I need to speak to the manager. She is expecting me." He held up his warrant card.

"Ah! That's why she buggered off!"

"Did she leave anything for me, D.S. Adams."

"Said to give you this." Jonathan glanced down at the handwritten note. There were five names. He requested the addresses and was surprised to learn they all shared a house on Jubilee Terrace.

"You won't get much out of them, only one speaks English, he translates for the others."

"East European?"

"Polish, they're the best workers."

"Tell your manager, I will need to speak to these people and expect her to call me with an arranged time we can come here to interview them. Failing that, we will interview them at their place of work. Won't look that good though, police interviewing your staff, word might get around." Turning on his heel, he made his way out of the building, the smell of the kebabs overwhelming his taste buds.

First port of call back at the office was the canteen. Having missed breakfast and lunch, he was famished.

Grabbing an artery clogging bacon roll, he walked up the stairs to the incident room. The smell of bacon arrived, just before the boss.

"Interview statements all sorted ready for the governor then?"

"Yes sir and I've checked the porter, Sidney White for previous. Had a breach of the peace in 1979. Given a conditional discharge. Sympathetic magistrate it seems."

"Ah, the winter of discontent, who didn't during the three day week? I've been busy too you know." There was Jake thinking otherwise.

"I've a list of possible cleaners, all Polish. According to the agency, only one of them speaks a little English. Still what's to understand dirt, broom, bucket?"

It had been a hectic few days; they had all worked very hard; needed to recharge their batteries. Adams and a couple of the other lads opted for the pub. He had fallen out once again with Doreen, the spectre of marriage once again rearing its ugly head, so no sex for him this evening. No reason for an early night. Jake opted to go straight home.

Chapter Five

Jake's weekend seemed to be over too quickly.

Saturday was spent with his partner at the gym, followed by lunch and a pint. It had to be his treat; it was him who had cancelled a number of their dates during the week. The afternoon was spent shopping for new Italian shoes and a rug for their sitting room.

In the evening they attended a dinner party with four of their closest friends, drank a considerable amount of wine and went home by taxi. Good company and excellent wine always made Jake horny. In the taxi, neither could contain themselves. Jake closed his eyes and lay back, as hands wandered inside his shirt and inner thigh. He hoped the driver had an open mind. They didn't even make it to the bedroom, had frantic sex in the hallway.

"I expect more of the same later!"

"I need it harder and longer next time. Use your fingers and mouth too!" He liked it when they both said what they wanted. Had never had that before in a relationship, it really turned him on.

Sunday lunch was spent with his mother. She had met his partner at a gallery opening, found they both enjoyed the same things, theatre, Italian cooking and shopping, just knew she had found the ideal partner for her Jake.

Although they had only been together for three months, Jake knew this was the one who would be the love of his life. They were already living together in a trendy loft apartment. The salary of a policeman only allowed him a section houseroom or stay at home; it was his partner who had the money.

The main topic of conversation over lunch had been his temporary promotion to the CID, they were both eager to hear what he was working on. He only gave them the briefest of details. An elderly man found dead in a hospital, possible suspicious death.

For Jonathan Adams however, the weekend was spent alone, poring over witness statements and files.

Doreen was still not talking to him. They had been together on and off for eight years. He would not commit, felt there might be somebody more deserving of him just around the corner. Doreen clung on hoping he would change, fearing he might be her only chance.

Uniform had taken statements from family members, including Wayne Dooley, the common law husband of his granddaughter, Shirley. Wayne had discussed with William Smith the possibility of him moving in with them, 'Shirley had always been his favourite, he said'.

Wayne had always admired William Smith, wanted a reputation like his, someone you didn't cross, saw it as his way of getting in with the family. Imagined himself as William Smith's right hand man; at least that was what the old man had told him. It seemed to Jonathan that the idea had been William Smith's all along.

Wayne had not yet spoken to Shirley; he thought it would be a nice surprise. They would be able to apply for a bigger place from the council. Shirley could apply for a Carers' Allowance, would be earning while at home looking after the kids. William Smith was well up for it. It was even his idea not to tell the rest of the family until it was all arranged. Since his beloved Elsie had died he told Wayne he had been very lonely, needed to be back in the bosom of his loving family.

Jean Smith's statement had been brief. She last saw her father two weeks ago. They had argued. Nothing-serious mind. He didn't like the meal she had brought over for him.

He hated the flat, wanted to be back in the house he shared with his wife. When she passed away, it became under occupied and he had to move out. No she hadn't realised he was so ill.

The brother who no longer kept in touch was proving elusive. The mobile number that Jean had given them belonged to an untraceable pay as you go. It seemed that he only kept in touch on his terms. The sister had not been too bothered. He would come to the funeral or not, made no difference to the rest of the family.

Staff Nurse Joyce Lloyd's statement was concise and to the point. She had been in her office doing paperwork. At around six o'clock, she heard one of the cleaners bustling about in the ward. Lisa was in the kitchen, making a brew and toast for them. Lisa and her had their tea and toast. Lisa took the cups back to the kitchen and she went to check patients' notes.

She became aware of a patient banging on the bathroom door about six fifty; she was able to pinpoint the time. They had a nil by mouth patient who might be able to squeeze a quick cuppa before meds. Saw water seeping under the door, so gained entry with a passkey. Mr Smith was submerged, she dragged him out, pulled the emergency cord and commenced mouth to mouth, and Lisa rushed to collect the resuscitation trolley. Sid White had come to collect a patient for theatre, realised what was happening and came over to assist.

Lisa, the trainee nurse had nothing more to add. Her statement read the same as Staff Nurse Lloyd's. Both wanted it down on record that they had been shorthanded on the ward. An Agency Nurse who should have been working the shift had not turned up. He scribbled a note to find out which agency and the name of the absent nurse.

The patients who had been awake at the time of the commotion had very little to add to the proceedings. The man needing the bathroom urgently had not seen the deceased enter the bathroom, was surprised to find it locked. He prided himself on being the first one to use it in the mornings, regular as clockwork he was.

In all the confusion, the cleaner slipped away unnoticed. Nurse Lloyd was unable to recall which of them had been working that morning. The hospital preferred male cleaners on the men's wards, but they took whoever was available.

The Primary Care Staff Agency had given him a list of

the five cleaners assigned to the Maritime Hospital for the early shift; two male, Adalbert Szymon and Maciej Waclaw and three females; Jolenta Bozena, Lydia Bozena and Florentyna Leonard. He just needed to establish which of them was assigned to Nelson Ward.

Pouring himself a generous glass of red wine, he began to go over the file on Freddie Smith again. Taken into care early on and a number of appearances in juvenile court before he hit the big time.

There was no mention of William Smith in the file. Elsie Smith seemed to have been the appropriate adult in most of the proceedings. Probably didn't give a toss, couldn't be bothered with him. Scant mention had been made of any siblings. Perhaps Elsie Smith had wanted to keep their names out of it, even warned Freddie of the consequences if they were dragged in. Strange that William Smith had put his son Freddie as next of kin when he had a daughter who obviously took care of him.

Chapter Six

It had been a good weekend. There had been great food, superior wine, the company of good friends and fantastic imaginative sex. Life Jake felt could not get much better than this. He walked through the double doors, whistling a tune.

"At least someone got laid. You're late," mumbled D S Adams, mainly because his weekend had been celibate.

"Sorry sir, traffic." It was all he could think of, when in fact, his partner had straddled him naked apart from chocolate covered nipples as the alarm woke him.

"Briefing in the incident room ten minutes, see where we're at."

Jake gathered up his reports and notes. Pleased he had set up the picture board Friday, before he left.

"What we have so far is one dead man, no clear motive. Any ideas? I'm prepared to listen to anything." All present looked down at their notes.

"Jake, what's your take on this?" Startled, he looked up, hadn't been listening, he was still in his warm bed licking chocolate off a pair of pert nipples.

Jake could think of nothing to add to the proceedings.

"Question is why not Jean Smith as next of kin? Freddie boy may know more than he's letting on. Certain people are not being honest with us, him included."

"Never!" came the surprised chorus.

"Yes really."

"The daughter, not sure if they got on. Gives the impression that she didn't care but still made sure he was clean and was fed."

"Any joy with the cleaners, sir?"

"We're waiting confirmation who was working the shift."

"Right people, you all have a copy of the post mortem findings. William Smith drowned. Marks on his neck and chest indicate that person or persons unknown kneeled on his chest. Doc' estimates it took only a few minutes. Been in the throes of sex, not self-service we understand. Probably eyes shut enjoying it, didn't have time to catch his breath. Yes I should have put it a little more delicately but this is a murder investigation. If, I have upset anyone, well tough. We need to find a motive."

Jake waited by his desk. He was to take part in the interview of Jean Smith. The drive to the Abelard Estate took no more than twenty minutes. Jean Smith lived in one of the smaller properties, in Elousie Gardens.

They took her by surprise when they appeared on her doorstep. Right arms extended holding warrant cards, Jake's the right one this time, they both offered their formal smiles.

"I wasn't expecting you. The policewoman already took my statement. I've people coming. It's not convenient."

"I'm sorry Madam, did one of my constables not let you know we were coming? It really won't take more than a few minutes." Jonathan Adams carefully wiped his feet on the mat outside and walked into the narrow hallway. Jake followed, mumbling apologies for the inconvenience.

"Lounge, through to the back? Cup of tea would be nice. Jake here's not good at making tea, needs lots of practice. You point out where it's kept, he can do the honours, while we chat. Be quicker then."

Jean pointed into the kitchen. Top left hand cupboard, mugs on the hook. He thanked her and filled up the kettle. When Adams closed the door he began to look around. Have a nose Adams had said.

"What exactly am I looking for sir?"

"When you see it you'll know. Sign of a good detective." All Jake could find in the kitchen were things that should be there crockery, food, and pedal bin.

Carefully, he lifted the lid, nothing but potato peelings and an empty cat food tin. Washing machine still had clothes waiting to be put out on the line. Loading up the tray, he knocked on the lounge door. Carefully placing the tray on a small coffee table, two cups only.

"There you go Ms Smith, tea, I hope it's strong enough. Would you mind very much if I used your bathroom?" He was gone before she had a chance to refuse.

Jake had no desire to make use of the toilet or hand basin, both in need of a good dose of bleach. Cardboard tubes from finished toilet rolls lined the windowsill, used tissues tossed carelessly onto the floor.

In the medicine cabinet, he found a half empty bottle of Prozac and a blister pack of Candesartan's which he remembered from his father's illness were for blood pressure problems. Jean Smith didn't look the sort of person to require blood pressure medicine. Flushing the toilet, he wandered out on to the landing. There were two bedrooms. One was in use as a bedroom, while the other was clearly a junk room.

He stepped back quickly when he heard the front door slam.

"'Shirl' is that you? The police are here asking questions about your granddad." Jean shouted a warning to her daughter. Jake noticed her hesitate at the sitting room door before entering.

Shirley Smith was a younger version of her mother just as thin and careworn.

"'Shirl' I was just telling them, we don't know nothing about granddad Bill. You hardly seen him at all, except when Wayne dragged you up the hospital. First time in ages you seen him, I just told 'em that." Jean's voice had a panicky edge to it. Staring intently at her daughter, willing her to keep quiet, fearful she may blurt out the wrong thing. Adams stood and smiled, holding out his hand.

"Ms Smith, may I call you Shirley? Are you aware that your partner Wayne Dooley was making arrangements for your grandfather to move in with you and your family?" The look of horror on their faces told him they had no idea.

"Apparently, he was going to apply for larger council accommodation and also a carers' allowance for you Ms Smith."

"The bastard, anything just so he don't have to lift a

finger and work."

"Mum!" Shirley angrily snapped. "That's my Wayne you're talking about."

"I had no idea but I'm sure he would have told me eventually." She recovered well from the question.

"Would there have been a problem with the arrangement?" Shirley glanced across at her mother.

"Well no, I don't think so. Definitely no."

"What about you Ms Smith. You never thought about taking your father in?"

"I have met someone, a good bloke, Sanj's his name. Drives a taxi. Him and Dad would not have got along. I told Dad I was moving away, making a fresh start. He would have wanted to stay close to his friends, any ways."

"Well thank you both for your time. We can show ourselves out."

Jonathan motioned to Jake they were leaving. At the door, he stopped a moment. From the back room came the muffled sound of raised voices. The granddaughter had no idea of the arrangement between Wayne and William Smith.

"William Smith's flat is just around the corner. I've arranged for a Housing Officer to meet us outside." They pulled up behind a dark grey Fiesta, the driver got out as they pulled up behind him.

"Foster, Mike Foster. Understand you want to look in Mr Smith's flat?"

"Yes we do. Model tenant?" Mike Foster laughed sarcastically.

"We had the papers ready to apply to the court for a possession order. Non-payment of rent and harassment of an Asian neighbour."

"A very difficult man to deal with?"

"Most of the time he was under the influence, sometimes drink, sometime cannabis or both. Jean, his daughter, she tried her best but really he was just not a nice person at all. Even she had enough. Stopped mediating on his behalf."

The filthy floor was strewn with half eaten takeaways

and empty beer cans. The bedroom no better. Bedding was pulled back. Dirty stained sheets lay rumpled on the double bed. In the kitchen, used crockery was piled up in the sink, the bin overflowing.

"There wasn't a problem when his daughter used to visit but she's not been around for months. According to Mr Smith she was thinking of moving away, wanted to know if he could have her house. Good riddance he said, going off with one of them. As I said, not a nice man."

"Thank you for your help. I think I've seen enough for the time being."

"We need to get in and clean up. Voids cost money."

"We are investigating a suspicious death and you will have the property back when we have finished, not before." As they left, Adams arranged to collect the keys later in the afternoon for a more detailed investigation.

Jonathan Adams had borrowed WPC Julie Burton, had applied to have her on the team for the investigation. Julie was an ambitious copper with an intuitive mind. If there was something of significance in the flat she would find it. Jake was assigned to accompany her.

"At least I'm letting you both have some lunch before you go. Shouldn't think you would want any after."

Jake warned Julie of the unpleasant smell that would greet them.

"Don't worry Jake, I live at home with three brothers, that sort of smell is the norm in our house."

Chapter Seven

The single occupancy block built in the sixties needed some attention. Out the back was a communal garden littered with rubbish and broken glass. Quite a few used needles too by the look of it. A wooden gate with missing and damaged slats led from the car park to the front of the building. Here could be found a long strip of grass, used as a dog's toilet.

The rusted, ill-fitting metal window frames desperately needed replacing. It had a flat roof and part of the guttering missing. Jake was pleased he didn't have to live there. With only the key to the deceased's front door they buzzed a couple of the other flats to gain entrance.

According to uniform most of the other tenants were like William Smith, older single men. Some had mental health issues, drug and alcohol dependency. Many distrusted the police. The address of the block was well known to uniform. Julie herself had called around on a number of occasions. A couple of other tenants she knew were under supervision orders.

Smith's flat looked even worse with the late afternoon sun struggling to penetrate the grimy windows. The electricity had been cut off so Julie pulled back the filthy curtains to gain more light. Jake had left the front door open to allow for some much needed fresh air.

Being the senior officer on scene, Jake gave himself the task of sorting through the mail and gave the unenviable task of looking through the rubbish to Julie.

"Julie, he may have been a user so be careful."

"Always am."

With the aid of a groundsheet spread out on the floor, she efficiently sorted the rubbish into two piles, one to go back into the trash and the other pile worth a look.

Both were careful not to sit on the settee or armchair. The smell of cannabis permeated the fabric.

Jake quickly sorted the usual mail of threatening letters

from the utility companies. He threw the junk mail to one side. Julie looked at him.

"You know Jake, you can tell a lot about a person by the sort of junk mail he receives?" Embarrassed, he collected it all together and began sorting through.

Along with the usual offers for low interest rate credit cards, there was a mail shot regarding holidays in Thailand and the Far East.

"Julie, look what do you make of these?" In the bottom of a sideboard, Jake had found an old metal biscuit tin full of black and white photographs. He flicked through them.

One pictured a young William Smith with an even younger Jean Smith sitting on his knee. She looked to be nine or ten years old. He had one arm around her shoulders, holding a bottle of ale, the other hand resting across her legs. In another snapshot, a young Jean was at the seaside, wearing only a pair of wool knickers. She was digging in the sand with bucket and spade. William Smith was kneeling to one side helping. A few were of a very young Freddie Smith with an even younger little girl, probably the sister Mary.

"I think we need to take these in for the boss. Make sure they are all logged."

Jake thought they had seen enough, suggested they return to the station.

Julie asked Jake to hang on; she had an idea and went into the bedroom. Lifting the mattress, she found what she was looking for. A hole had been ripped on the underside of the mattress. Poking around in the hole, she found it. The text was in German but from the pictures, it was obvious that William Smith had a liking for prepubescent children.

"How on earth did you know where to look?"

"Told you, I come from a family of brothers. I knew all their secret hiding places."

Jake was seeing Julie Burton in a new light. Now he understood Adam's reason for having her on the team.

"Do you know what is missing Jake? Where are the pictures of his 'beloved' Elsie? Finding a magazine like this, there's got to be more and videos too I shouldn't wonder, we just need to find them. So Jake, where'd you hide your dirty books from your parents?"

Jake coloured slightly, remembering the large air vent in his room that held all his secrets. Julie checked the videotapes stacked up beside the TV. The covers showed the usual tapes a man of his age would be interested in; war films, the odd John Wayne cowboy movie. She opened one at random, slipped it into the machine and pressed play. The first few minutes were of John Wayne surveying his cattle, rounding them up. The tape then went blank for a moment.

The tape changed from colour to grainy black and white. A little girl of around five years old, dressed in high heels, was hitching up an adult black negligee, in order not to trip over. Her lips appeared dark and full, probably red from badly applied lipstick and her eyelids looked a dark garish colour. She was looking directly into the camera, trying desperately not to cry.

"I don't want to play this any more. I want Mummy." She began to wail. An arm came into view and a hand slapped her sharply across the face.

"Stop the tape, go back a few seconds. Stop there."

Although the hand was slightly out of focus, Jake could make out the word 'love' across the knuckles of the slapping hand.

"Bag the lot. We'll take them with us." Jake was eager to get back to the station, show the boss what they had uncovered.

"Jake, I may be wrong." She hesitated, unsure if she should continue.

"No don't worry, it's nothing. Just being paranoid."

"What is it? Your intuition has been good so far. I trust your instincts." Julie beamed at the compliment.

"Well this block, full of single men. You don't suppose that a number of them were into this with Smith? Oh, don't mind me, I'm seeing conspiracies where they aren't any." Jake looked at her in admiration, the idea had not even occurred to him.

"Might be worth running all their names through HOLMES when we get back. Also contact the Probation Service, check if they've dumped any paedophiles on us in the last few months."

Back at the station, Jake recounted to Jonathan Adams what they had found, making sure that Julie was given due credit. Jonathan admired his honesty and wondered if perhaps he should have Julie rather than Jake as his assistant.

Find the motive and you will find the perpetrator, one of the first rules taught to Adams by his old retired governor, a thief taker of the old school.

Adams also managed to second Sergeant Gill Cole. Although now part of the Youth Offending Team, she had previously worked with abused children. Her input would be invaluable.

"Sir, what about Jean Smith? Are we going to bring her in for questioning?"

"I'm going to leave her to sweat for a while. Make her think we accepted all she told us. I want a little more background. Anyway, we're going to be busy."

*****

Jonathan Adams nodded off on the journey down, snoring loudly. Jake drove in silence. The new bridge to the Isle of Sheppey was now open, the crossing faster. He marvelled at the engineering that had taken only two years to complete, at least that's what had been written on the huge billboard.

Six days since the murder and they still had nobody in the frame. It was important that the motive be established very soon. They had made significant strides with the find of the videos and pornographic magazines.

Jonathan Adams woke with a start as Jake took the speed bumps into the prison car park a little too quickly. Adams wiped his mouth where he had begun to dribble, embarrassed, hoped he had not been snoring.

The officer on the gate was the same one, recognised them immediately but still insisted on following protocol.

"That's the trouble with Prison Officers Jake, they're too stupid to become coppers, and this is the best they can do."

Freddie Smith was none too happy. He had no option but to agree to see them otherwise it would look bad. He was due for parole soon, didn't want to jeopardise his chances.

"So Freddie, tell me about your old man. Get on well did you?"

"He was my old man, what else is there to say. A bastard most of the time."

"Have you any idea why you were registered as his next of kin?"

"Nope. Did he leave me anything? I ain't got no money to pay for a funeral."

"When did you last have contact with him?"

"Can't remember."

"What about your siblings."

"What?"

"Family. Your twin sister Jean, were you close? Your sister Mary, how did you get on with her? What about your younger brother, Michael is it?"

"They was family, didn't choose them, they didn't choose me. Jean and me, we're not close. The old man preferred her when we was younger. Beat the living daylights out of me. Weren't allowed near her much; none of us was. Mary, now she was much more understanding." Freddie closed his eyes and smiled to himself.

"Understanding in what way then Freddie?" Adams asked in a conversational tone.

"That was a misunderstanding, she's stupid you know, never knows what's what."

"Your life, full of misunderstandings is it Freddie?"

"Governor said I didn't have to talk to you without representation if I don't want to and I don't want to any more. I've finished talking unless I got my solicitor here." Freddie

Smith scowled and turned his back on them.

Adams nodded to the Prison Officer who escorted Freddie out. Leaving formalities complete, they walked back to the car.

"Well that was a wasted journey, sir."

"You drive, I need thinking time."

Sleeping time more like.

"Before you leave this evening, I want a quick update with everyone in the Incident Room, the board needs updating." Just because Adams had no social life.

"So did either of you find a will, insurance policies anything like that?"

"No sir, apart from what we logged and brought back with us that was it really."

"Jake, make a note to contact that Housing Officer in the morning, see if Mr Smith had a solicitor. If he was being taken to court for repossession he may have got hold of one under Legal Aid. Do we know if Social Services were involved with the family when they were younger?"

One of the team stood up, reading from his notebook.

"Yes sir. Social Services were involved with the family in regard to Mary. Mary was found unconscious in a bath of cold water. Almost drowned. There was speculation at the time whether or not it was accidental."

"Just like William Smith."

"Mary was being looked after by William Smith on the night. Elsie the wife, returned home from her evening cleaning job, found him drunk in a chair. His clothes were wet, she rushed into the bathroom, found Mary unconscious. Paramedics revived her at the scene. He claimed he had put her to bed. She must have been sleepwalking, got back in the bath."

"Elsie gave up her evening job and they agreed to let the family stay together but put Mary on the 'At Risk' Register."

Jake managed to escape after an hour. His partner was working late this evening. If he hurried, he would be the first home for a change.

Chapter Eight

Jonathan Adams had been in his office for the past hour. The doughnuts he had purchased for the early risers all eaten.

Despite making the effort not to be too late last night, Doreen was still demanding their relationship be put on a legal footing. Again he prevaricated, ended the evening at his own home alone, another celibate night…

Jake and Julie breezed in, surprised to find the gaffer already there, sifting through updated CRIS reports.

"Glad you could both find the time to join me!" Jonathan Adams was in a foul mood. Both Jake and Julie mumbled apologies even though they were early. Over the next fifteen minutes the remainder of the team began wandering in. Adams banged on the desk to get their attention. The quicker the briefing was finished; the sooner tasks could be allocated. He began by outlining his thoughts so far.

The time and place of the killing could not have been spur of the moment. It had taken planning, meticulous timing, allowed very little margin of error. There was a degree of recklessness, the ward being a fairly public place. The person needed to know hospital procedure, be able to blend in unnoticed. They began to nod their agreement.

They still needed to understand how it was carried out. At that time of the morning, there would be few people on the ward. A stranger would be noticed, so the murderer must have looked as though he or she belonged, right place, right time.

There were a number of possible motives. William Smith's own sexual proclivities or, the murder could also be down to Freddie Smith's activities. Freddie was involved with drugs and debt collection. With Freddie in prison, killing his old man would be the next best thing.

"A week. The trail is beginning to go cold. We're no nearer a suspect."

"Julie, I need you to come with me for the interview of

53

Mary Smith. Spoke to her Social Worker last night. Mary's unsettled by men, so you will be interviewing her, I'll just be in the background. Any questions anyone? Check your emails, you all have your assignments for today."

"Change into civvies. Julie."

Jake was disappointed but understood. There were times when gender did make a difference.

*****

The house where Mary lived was a large Edwardian semi, set a little back from the road. The front garden had become overgrown. Thick foliage hung over the path. The door was opened before they had even knocked.

"I've been expecting you. Jean rang."

She explained Mary's problems, her autism and difficulties interacting with strangers, particularly men.

"She's fine with our male staff, the milkman, postman and our old gardener, had time to get to know them."

"I told Mary you were coming, not sure how much she understood. Some days she can be quite lucid, others, she's in her own little world."

"Does she get many visitors?"

"Her sister Jean and niece Shirley visit most days and a brother visits but I've never met him. Always comes early morning, when the night sleeper is still on duty."

"Don't suppose you have an address for him?"

"Sorry. Next of kin is down as Jean Smith, other emergency contact is Shirley Smith."

They were escorted to the residents' lounge, Adams hung back letting Julie take the lead. Staring out the window was a delicate looking young woman. Face covered in freckles, the sunlight glinting on her red hair, a strand of which she was twisting around her finger, a delicate beauty about her.

"Hello Mary, my name is Julie, may I talk with you?"

She turned at the sound of a voice. Clutching a tattered

54

knitted doll, she began to rock to and fro on the chair. Julie gave her a reassuring smile, taking great care not to invade her private space.

"Jean told us where to find you." At the mention of Jean's name, she looked up, made eye contact for a split second.

Julie chatted about the birds in the garden, her pretty doll and anything she could think of to gain her trust.

"It's the autism. If she doesn't want to let you in, there's nothing to be done."

"Do you keep a record of who visits and when here?"

"Of course. Health and Safety Regulations."

"May we have a copy of all visitors to Mary over the past month?"

"I'm not sure. I'll have to take advice and get back to you."

"You do that." Julie thanked her for her time, making sure to say her goodbyes to Mary.

Back in the car a thought occurred to her.

"Sir, do you think they use the same cleaning agency as the hospital?" He knew her secondment had been a good choice.

"Have another look at the report on Mary when we get back. Is her lack of understanding and communication permanent?"

Back at the station, they found Jake hunched over his computer, a pile of printouts by his side. Adams asked him for an update.

"I've run a check of other tenants at McArthur House. A couple of drunk and disorders, non-payment of fines, the usual. One tenant George Parker is on the sex offenders' register, has been since it was set up. Gill was wondering when Julie would be back, there are a lot of tapes still to go through."

"Right then Julie, get yourself some coffee, put the details of Mary Smith's interview into the system. Print up a copy for the governor. Then assist Gill with the rest of the tapes."

"Where shall I put the broom when I remove it from my person boss?" Adams grinned; he liked a girl with a sense of humour.

The cleaners had arrived from the agency, were kicking their heels in reception.

Jake and Jonathan Adams, together with an interpreter took them to the interview room.

Two had been shifted in for that day, Jolenta Bozena, and Maciej Waclaw. Maciej spoke a little English. Jolenta seemed unsure, looked to Waclaw when questioned.

Both confirmed they had been told they would be starting later on that particular Wednesday. Staff training the manager said. Maciej thought they just didn't want to pay them the full amount. They did not make it in, they received a call from the hospital, there had been an incident.

Jonathan asked if starting late was a regular occurrence. Waclaw shrugged his shoulders. They gained very little else. If there was a cleaner in that morning, they were bogus. Adams concluded the interview, said they may be needed again, leaving them with a uniform constable to write up what they knew.

In the incident room Gill Upton and Julie Burton were having a break, teasing Jake, about his love life. They laughed as he threatened to report them for sexual harassment. Adams would love them to sexual harass him, it had been a few weeks and he was getting more frustrated. Doreen was holding out for marriage, commitment, the whole works.

Realising he was there, they both stood up. Embarrassed he might have heard.

"Sir we have finished reviewing the tapes brought in. Three were not what they seemed. One was in German, the usual; S & M, adult bondage; one involved very young boys and girls, both of them commercially made. The third was definitely home made. The quality was not that good. I think it might have been transferred from reel to reel." Adams was impressed at her thoroughness.

"Julie seems to think that the young girl featured may be Jean Smith. I will have our technical guys print up stills. I'll email my report and recommendations to you, should have it by late tomorrow. I'm in court in the morning; otherwise, it would be sooner."

"No that's fine. Send it to Julie; she'll be covering this part of the enquiry."

Jake ran through the information he had on George Parker. Like William Smith, he had only recently become a tenant in the block. They were not known acquaintances as far as he was able to ascertain, but they could have made contact, both being recent tenants.

Adams requested more information on George Parker.

"We need to go back to the murder scene. It's important we find how they got in and out of Nelson Ward unobserved."

Chapter Nine

Jean loved Leysdown, came down as often as she could. Even visited Freddie once. The Visiting Order he sent enabled her to get some travel money from the social. But then he wanted her to bring in Mary. Mary had been through enough with him and so she never visited again.

Although the afternoon sun was warm, the breeze off the water was keen and she snuggled down in the shelter.

"I couldn't believe it when the old Bill turned up. Thought we'd been rumbled before we could do it. You said we would do him Friday. It was all arranged. At least when they turned up and said he was dead I looked really shocked, didn't even need to pretend."

"We agreed not to meet up until it was all over. You have put us all at risk."

The smartly dressed man, sitting the other side of the glass shelter was reading the Daily Telegraph. A casual observer would not realise they were communicating.

"Why did you bring it forward? We agreed I would do him."

"I didn't bring it forward. Somebody got to him before we could. When I know what happened, you will know, in the meantime, wait until I contact you."

"Jean! Jean!" At the sound of her name she looked toward the beach. Jumping up and down excitedly was Mary brandishing a large conch shell. She waved back then turned round to continue her conversation. But he was gone. She gathered up their belongings and called to Mary. It was time for them to catch the bus; they could not miss their connection back to London. Mary's bottom lip began to quiver. Jean hated to see her sad, promised Mary they would come again very soon.

On the way to the bus stop, she stopped to buy Mary a candy floss, what the hell, she would have one herself, remind her of the time when they all came for a holiday without him and were truly happy. William Smith had been sent down for non-payment of a fine, seven days the magistrate gave him. The social had put Elsie in touch with a charity that provided breaks for deprived families. Mum, her, Mary and Mickey came down here. Freddie didn't come. Mum wouldn't let him, too like his father. He stayed with a friend.

For that short week they were able to pretend they were a proper normal family. Jean never wanted to leave but they had to go back. While Mum was propping up the bar at the camp social club letting her hair down, Mickey, me and Mary would be sitting outside on the grass with the normal kids, drinking Vimto and eating crisps.

One of these days, Mickey said things would be different. Mickey had big plans, was getting out as soon as he could. Promised he would make it better for us, he kept his word but at a price. We weren't to know where he lived or what he was doing with his life. Our only communication with him was through the mobile phone he gave me.

*****

The viewing room was small and unbearably hot. The operator had set aside a desk and monitor for Jake.

Adams had decided not to go for a seizure warrant unless there was something of interest on the CCTV tapes. The hospital was dotted with signs warning CCTV is watching you but in reality, only the camera in Accident and Emergency was fully operational.

The first tape was a time-lapse overview of the car park.

"I know you're looking for around six but run it from midnight. Couple having it away against one of the pillars in the covered section. Difficult to see who they are mind." Jake ignored the advice and started it from around five o'clock.

His interest was aroused by a dark coloured saloon tucked in the corner of the staff designated area. The driver took great care not to look directly toward the camera.

"Do you recognize the car or driver?"

"No mate but I'll print a still off it if you want." Running on the tape, Jake was unable to pick him up again. He began viewing the A & E tape.

The picture quality was better, more outside lighting on the forecourt. Faces could be recognized. Jake scanned the screen, looking for the male on the previous tape, the driver of the saloon. The entrance door to the emergency department was the only one open this early in the morning and he would have needed to use it to gain access to the hospital. He did not appear.

"Staff on early shift. How do they enter the hospital?"

"Round the back of the building. They need a swipe card."

"Where would I get a copy printout of swipe cards?"

"Not sure, check with Ms Jones, most things go by her first."

Jake wandered out to the main car park to get some fresh air. He walked to the spot where the dark saloon had been parked. He wanted to check it if would be possible to reach the fire escape outside Nelson Ward unobserved by CCTV.

Keeping close to the wall of the main building he evaded the camera until that is he reached the Ambulance Bay. Here he was in direct line of sight of the camera. The siren of an incoming ambulance startled him, almost knocked him down. However, skirting behind the vehicle, unseen he was able to make his way to the fire escape. It could be done, but how could you be sure that there would be an ambulance to cover your tracks?

Given the opportunity, this could have been the way the killer entered the ward. But that would mean more than one person involved because try as he might, he could not gain entry from outside the building.

*****

Jonathan Adams was looking forward to his meeting

with Ms Jones; hoping to take her out for a quiet lunch, even perhaps ask her out for dinner. He was not best pleased to see Jake walking down the corridor towards him.

"Sir, I think I may have found something but I need to look at a copy of the swipe card report for the day of the murder. Apparently most paperwork goes by Ms Jones first."

"I think I can manage to do that. Go get a coffee, I'll come and find you when I've finished."

Tamara Jones face fell as she turned into the corridor.

"Sergeant Andrews, what can I do for you?" Adams smiled, pretended not to notice she had forgotten his name.

"Just a few questions Ms James, it shouldn't take long."

She unlocked her door, ushered him in.

"It's Jones, Sergeant. You will need to be quick, I have meetings."

"Adams. That's my name but you can call me Jonathan, Tamara." He liked that name, classy.

"You can call me Ms Jones and preferably make an appointment before you turn up. I just can't drop everything to speak to you."

"I think you will find you can, particularly as I am conducting a murder enquiry. If necessary, we can speak down the station, away from all your distractions."

"Sorry, it's just that I am under a lot of pressure. Year end budgets, you understand."

"There was me thinking you were under pressure to find out what happened on Nelson Ward, last Wednesday." She had the grace to look sheepish.

"So Ms Jones, tell me a little about yourself. Are you spoken for?"

"What has this got to do with the unfortunate incident?"

"Absolutely nothing, I'm just interested."

"I do not want to appear rude, Jonathan is it, but you're just not my type." Realising there was no chance of a date he decided to stick to formalities, requesting copies of various reports. He also showed her the printout of the hooded man.

"Really, I can't help you. I don't recognize the man.

Even his own mother would struggle to recognize him from that photo. Anything else, speak to my secretary. I really have to go I have an important meeting."

Jonathan Adams rose to leave but advised they would need to speak again. He no longer had any ambitions where Ms Jones was concerned but equally, he would not be summarily dismissed.

"Bloody woman, who does she think she is?"

Jake had just sat down to enjoy his Mocha coffee when his mobile went off.

"Where the bloody hell are you? I'm waiting by the car, haven't got all day." The counter assistant took pity on him, transferred his drink into a disposable cup.

Adams was still in a bad mood as they walked through the station reception area. Here they were detained by the counter clerk. It seemed that the Duty Sergeant needed to speak to them as a matter of urgency.

"Whose feathers have you ruffled then Jake?"

"Get on with it man. We're busy people."

"Seems a body has been found by Kent Police. They ran the name through the system and Jake here, well his name came up as showing an interest."

"Do we get a prize for guessing?" Embarrassed, the Duty Sergeant mumbled something about thinking you're better than us.

"Parker, George Parker. Can you give Detective Inspector Spencer a call as soon as?" Jake took the note and thanked the Duty Sergeant. When the investigation was over, he would probably have to return to uniform and it wouldn't do to take sides.

Chapter Ten

Jake was unhappy that Adams was to collect him from his apartment. Adams made it his job to look into the private lives of those working for him, hated surprises.

He was downstairs outside the entrance before the car had even turned around.

"Must be paying you too much if you can afford to live here or is there something I should know?"

"Sir I've no idea what you are talking about."

"You a toy boy then Mortimer? I should imagine you would appeal to the older woman," Jake stammered.

"I, I share with my partner who earns a lot more than I do."

"Doesn't bother you that she's the breadwinner then?" He chose not to answer. Adams walked around the front of the car, handing the keys to Jake.

It was a fairly straight run, M2, M20, no little windy roads and they had left early to avoid heavy traffic. Adams insisted they stop at Clacketts Lane services so he could pick up a bacon roll. Jake kept his eyes on the road so he didn't have to watch Adams dripping butter and sauce down his chin. His partner's idea for them both to go vegetarian was looking more interesting by the minute.

Arriving at Sittingbourne Police Station they showed their warrant cards to the desk clerk who referred them to the desk sergeant.

"Not on my list."

Desk sergeants, thought Jake, the same attitude to CID no matter which station.

"Spence didn't say he was expecting visitors. We had a murder yesterday, he's over on the island."

"He does work out of Sittingbourne?"

"Course he does, they all do unless it's really big then they work out of Headquarters at Maidstone."

"Any chance you could call him to let him know we're here? He requested the meeting with us." Adams who had kept quiet, indigestion getting the better of him, lost patience.

"Just show us to his office, we'll wait there while you call him. If it's going to be a problem well then I can always ring my Chief Constable to liase with your Chief Constable. Don't know about yours but mine with be pissed off to get a call this time of the morning."

"Message from the desk sergeant, Inspector's on his way, about ten minutes."

Detective Inspector Dave Spencer was a little younger than Adams. It annoyed Adams that he had already been made an inspector. He wanted to know their interest in George Parker and why they had visited the island twice recently. Adams decided to be circumspect with his answers for the time being.

"Could I ask, how did he die and where exactly was the body found?"

"We are keeping certain facts out of the public domain. Attacked with a knife. Slashed quite a few times. Had he lived he would be singing soprano now. I'm waiting on an autopsy as to which stab was the fatal one."

Jake was furiously taking down notes.

"He was found on the shingle at Warden Point, one of the farthest points on the island, quite remote and a well hidden area. Any later and the body would have been washed away. Thank goodness for keen dog walkers. I don't think we were expected to find the body."

"How far is this Warden Point in relation to the prison complex?"

"Just over a mile." As a professional courtesy, he requested a copy of the autopsy, just in case there was a connection. Likewise, he would let the Kent Police have details of their investigation.

Dave Spencer arranged for a local patrol car to take them to the site. The driver was an islander, could answer any questions they may have and he would be able to track their movement on his patch.

From their vantage point they were able to see the prison complex.

"Could he have been meeting a prisoner unofficially?" The constable shrugged.

"Easy enough to sneak away. It has been known. Slip out give the wife or girlfriend one, lots of empty caravans during the week."

The patrol officer drove them around the perimeter of the prison complex, pointing out a number of locations where a prisoner could sneak out.

They returned to Sittingbourne to collect their own car. The desk sergeant, a little more respectful this time passed over an envelope containing copy preliminary statements, photos and other information the murder team thought would be useful.

"Sir, do you think this is connected to our murder?"

"Yes, course it is. George Parker and William Smith, living in the same block of flats, both interested in young children.

"Has the Paedophile Unit come back yet with information on nonce's on our patch?" Jake shook his head.

Julie was engrossed in setting up another white board in the incident room, didn't even look up when they came in.

"Seem to have a lot of potential suspects." Adams' voice startled her.

"I saw my life flash before me then, not a pretty sight, apart from the time I was thin." Jake loved her sunny nature and sense of humour.

"Not suspects sir, possible victims. They are taken from the video. This one here we're almost sure is Jean Smith. The three young lads we've no names for yet."

Adams stared, expecting one to be Freddie Smith, but no. They were around the ages of eight or nine, in various stages of undress. Gill Cole had selected the frames that would best identify the boys.

The abusers made sure they were not in a direct shot, but

there were still a couple of frames from which they could possibly be identified. Julie had placed these underneath.

On Adams' instruction, Jake set up another board with details of the George Parker murder. With all the team assembled, he began to outline what they knew about the new murder.

"George Parker, neighbour and possible friend of our victim, now himself deceased. The body found close to the prison housing Freddie Smith." A dissenting voice from the back complained they didn't need another body, still hadn't sorted out the one they already had. Adams assured them it was not their investigation. He needed them to take on board the information he was giving them as both murders were connected.

A nervous probationer stood awkwardly in the doorway coughing loudly to attract attention. Annoyed at being stopped in full flow Adams shouted at him.

"It'd better be important lad!"

"Sir, Sergeant Dexter thought you might want to know, Wayne Dooley's in the front office. He's brought in his documents, was stopped in Kent a few days ago, said you might be interested. Sergeant Dexter put him in interview room one." Dexter was an old school copper, worked by instinct.

*****

Just the usual stop and check they said. Pulled over at the lay-by after the bridge, he panicked. Told the officers it was his car but did not have the documents with him. He was requested to produce them at his nearest station within seven days. Now he had to admit that the car was not his and he had no tax or insurance. Truth be told, it had been brought to the scrap yard for disposal and he had taken advantage of the fact it was still a goer.

All this Wayne Dooley explained to Adams. A mate had

asked him to give a lift to a friend, paid him fifty quid for his trouble. He had two young kids as they well knew. The money would come in useful. Useful for the bookies thought Jake.

"The name of your mate would be helpful Mr Dooley."

"Can't see, as I just said he's a mate. I'm no grass." Adams looked at him and sighed. Wayne began to feel nervous, started to sweat, even though the room was cool.

Jake produced from the drawer two fresh tapes and placed them in the machine.

"I assume that Sergeant Dexter went through your rights with you regarding the failure to produce your documents Wayne." Adams already knew he hadn't had specifically requested that he didn't.

"Pity, you've been treated as a grieving relative up until now, but well I'm not so sure. Help works both ways. You help us and perhaps the paperwork on the car might be mislaid."

"I know my rights, I want a solicitor. I'm saying nothing else."

"You've not been inside yet have you Wayne? You might be back on the Isle of Sheppey sooner than you think. Still, good looking boy like you. You'll be just fine, someone will look out for you, one or two who will take a fancy to a good looking lad."

Wayne crumbled; Adams knew he would.

Chapter 11

An unmarked car had collected Wayne from his home. Thursday was his dole day and he was anxious to get it over with early. This also suited the Kent detective.

"I'd like to sit in on the interview it you don't mind. Dooley figures in both our investigations."

Wayne and Shirley had talked most of the night. More like begging on his part to be given yet another chance. She had rung her mum as soon as he returned from the station. Jean ranted at him, hadn't they enough problems already. They wore him down, better a grass than a lonely bloke living in a grotty bed-sit, never seeing his kids.

"I ain't no grass you got to understand and I ain't no murderer either. If I go down, Shirley won't stand by me. She's already said, that's why I'm here." Jake nodded, said he understood, told him how much they all appreciated his co-operation.

Detective Inspector Dave Spencer of the Kent Police and Detective Sergeant Jonathan Adams entered the interview room. Jake stood to allow both men to conduct the interview. They informed Wayne it was to be an informal interview, at this stage.

"Jake here, I hope he's been looking after you Wayne. Tea or coffee?"

"No, I mean yes, I've no complaints. I ain't got a solicitor with me. I've done nothing wrong, just give a bloke a lift that's all." Adams smiled and introduced Dave Spencer.

"Mr Dooley, or may I call you Wayne? Have my colleagues told you anything yet?"

"Just my ticket might get lost if I help you, but I ain't a grass."

Dave Spencer pushed a photo across the table.

"Wayne, was this the man you gave a lift to?" He glanced at it briefly, unsure whether he should tell the truth.

"Might be, not too good at faces." Adams pushed his

chair backwards. Wayne looked up in alarm, saw the steely determination in Adams face.

"Yes," he mumbled under his breath. "But I don't really know him. A mate just said he had a friend who needed a lift down to Sheppey. He was staying for a couple of days and was going to let me know when he needed collecting."

"Your mate Wayne. Has he a name?"

"I ain't…"

"No grass, yes I think we have established that. Have you made further contact with this mate who asked you to do the favour?"

"No."

"Is it perhaps," Adams smiled at him.

"It is because he had recently died? William Smith asked you to do the favour didn't he?"

Wayne looked up and nodded. Relieved they already knew and he didn't need to become a grass. He told them where he had dropped him off, the same place he wanted to be collected from, Blue Town. Didn't chat on the way down but that was okay, Wayne found it difficult to make small talk at the best of times. They left the room, Jake was to take his statement , then he was free to go.

"What about my ticket then?"

"What ticket?"

"The one I. Gotcha!" Anyway with the car now crushed, there was no physical evidence, a conviction would have been questionable.

"Wayne, one last question. Did you get the scotch for William Smith while he was in the hospital?" Wayne shook his head.

So George Parker was an associate of William Smith, a mate if Wayne was to be believed.

Adams stared at the incident boards. Something was there he just couldn't see it at the moment. They were into the second week of the investigation. If they didn't get a significant breakthrough soon, his team would be cut.

Detective Chief Inspector Fisher had put his reputation

on the line by allowing him to run the investigation. If he failed, he would be spending the rest of his service as a lowly sergeant, most probably in uniform. He had to succeed if only to prove to that pillock Bryan Low that he was more of a detective that he could ever hope to be.

The collating of the reports from Tammy Jones, Adams put in the capable hands of Jimmy Benton. The Met', like other Forces often used retired officers to review cases that had been going for a while. Although not technically a cold case, Jimmy and Adams were friends and he called in a favour.

Jimmy had been a methodical dogged detective, picking up on clues that others missed. Adams was hoping Jimmy would provide him with the elusive evidence he desperately needed.

"So you're Jonno's new whipping boy then!" He proffered his hand.

"Jimmy Benton." Jake shook hands and smiled.

"Thinks you've got the makings of a good detective providing you listen and learn. I told him the same when he wasn't much older than you."

"So, you've known DS Adams man and boy. Bet you know a few of his exploits and secrets!" Jimmy Benton laughed.

"Involved in most of them with him." Jimmy had been looking at the hospital swipe card report, it made interesting reading.

Jimmy and Jake compared it to the duty rosters for that day. There were a few members of staff who had arrived early but were not shifted in. Of particular interest was Jones T. On the day in question, the swipe card had been used to enter and exit within six minutes.

"Jake you and Julie go pick up Ms Jones, bring her here, see if she's still full of herself after we've had words." This was turning into a good day after all.

*****

Tammy Jones was most indignant at being bothered yet again. She informed Jake that it bordered on harassment. Insisted on telephoning her boss who would sort out the mess. But Jake was firm.

"Not a happy lady." Julie informed Adams, when they returned.

"She's in reception at the moment, where do you want her put?" Adams decided interview room three would be ideal. Julie asked if he was sure. It had no air conditioning and only a tiny window. Adams wanted to intimidate Ms Jones, not that he was one to bear a grudge.

"If she wants a coffee let her have one but nothing else."

On instruction from Adams, Jake ran Ms Jones' details through the computer. She was not the prim and proper lady she purported to be, quite wild in her youth, been cautioned for substance use. Jonathan doubted her present employers would be aware of this.

Adams let her sweat for a while before he went with Jake to conduct the interview.

"You have no right, this is harassment, you will pay dearly for this."

"Sorry to have kept you waiting Ms Jones, shall we get started?" Adams placed the open file on the table.

"So what were you doing at the hospital at five am on Wednesday morning?"

"I have absolutely no idea what you are on about. I work office hours."

"Your swipe card says you entered at five and left minutes later."

"That's just not possible." Tammy Jones stopped mid sentence.

"Remembering are we?" Suddenly she seemed very unsure of herself, all arrogance gone.

"I can explain," she blustered.

Tammy Jones had been mugged Tuesday evening as she walked to her car. Been out for the night with a friend. Adams asked for her friend's name. For a moment the arrogant Tammy returned, said her friend was nothing to do with the mugging and was not prepared to name the person concerned, at this stage.

The mugger had frightened, not hurt her. Being unsure whether or not she was over the limit, she drove carefully home, deciding not to involve the police, cancelled her bank and credit cards the same evening.

She arrived at work on Wednesday morning, earlier than usual, fully intending to cancel her swipe card and arrange a replacement. Fortunately, she had no need. A package had been left for her at the front desk, her empty purse. Together with a note, explaining they had left it at the hospital as a swipe card for the Memorial was the only clue as to the owner. In all the confusion concerning the death of Mr Smith, it had slipped her mind completely. The receptionist could vouch for the chain of events.

"Why cancel your cards Tuesday evening but do nothing about the lost swipe card?"

"I have just explained, if you took the trouble to listen properly. I would have sorted it out as soon as I reached the office but it was found."

Adams wanted to charge her with wasting police time.

"Don't suppose you kept the note?" Jake enquired.

"No reason to, the person did not leave a name or address where I could write to thank them."

"They'll probably want to thank you," mumbled Adams under his breath. Pushing back his chair, he picked up the report and left the WPC to take down her statement.

"Is he always such a bastard?"

"Don't know," she answered, "haven't worked here long enough to have an opinion."

Adams sighed, another dead end.

The catering supervisor on the early shift had used the same entry door a few minutes after Ms Jones' swipe card had been used. Jake had interviewed him. As he said, it was over a week ago but he was sure that it was not Tammy Jones. He knew her quite well they had crossed swords, would have remembered. He also told Jake that had it been a stranger he would have remembered that as well. So early in the morning, he just couldn't recall who it had been.

Unfortunately, the door was for staff only. Budget restraints meant it had not been covered by a camera.

Chapter 12

Jonathan Adams had been looking forward to this evening. Doreen said she would prepare him a very special meal, an evening he would never forget. The case had kept him busy, needed to make up for his neglect.

He was running late, ended up with garage forecourt flowers but at least he had a decent bottle of red. Doreen was a good cook when she set her mind to it. He called a cab. Overnight parking around Doreen's flat was 'residents only' and he had been clamped once before, an experience he was not keen to repeat.

A tanned Doreen greeted him with a kiss. She looked different, excited and tanned. Her hair braided, the beads jangling, he followed her back up the stairs. She prattled on about her few days away. The traditional Gambian meal was not to his liking but the red was excellent and there would be sex at the end of the evening.

"The thing is Jonny, I've met somebody over the Internet we have been emailing for quite a few months. I went to stay with him and well, it was just love at first sight." Doreen stammered anxious to get the words out as quickly as she could.

"I'm going to marry Mohammed. He's six foot, incredibly handsome, has his own goat herd. I've only come back to tidy up my affairs. Let's face it, it's not as if we were going anywhere. He is a little younger than me but the sex is just incredible."

She had never told him their sex together was incredible.

"I really want us to stay friends. We were together a long time. I'm sure you wish me well." Actually, he didn't.

"No sex tonight then?" Doreen looked at him aghast. She would never she said betray her betrothed.

Single again, reasonably fit and handsome, all his own teeth. Just the wrong side of forty but with maturity came experience. For a man who had just been dumped he was in excellent high spirits. It galled him however to be dumped for a goat herder.

He walked towards the taxi rank. What he needed was a woman of independent means who understood the problems of his job; failing that a young nubile bimbo looking for a father figure, with independent means obviously.

"Where to mate?" Giving the driver his address, he settled down in the back, turned on his mobile to check for messages. He had quite a few, including two from Jimmy Benton.

Jimmy requested he call by if he wasn't busy, had found one or two things that might be of interest. Adams checked his watch, just after nine, still early for Jimmy. He asked the driver to stop at an off-licence. Strong beer was Jimmy's poison.

Jimmy still lived in the two up Victorian terraced house bought by his parents. Two divorces had left him with very little spare cash. Had he not inherited the house a few years back he could well have been living on the streets.

"You could have called to say you were on your way. I might have been entertaining." Adams looked at Jimmy, bare feet, faded jogging bottoms and a tatty polo shirt.

"I seriously doubt that. I have emergency supplies so do I get to come in then?" Jimmy stood aside, relieving Adams of his heavy load. Opening the can he took a deep swig. Adams knew the way.

The kitchen table was piled high with files and scraps of notepaper. Adams made to move some files from a chair.

"No don't move them, I have a system, I'll lose my train of thought."

"I think you've already lost it mate, you need to get a life outside the job." What was he saying, he was just as bad, was here with him wasn't he.

"Julie Burton, nice lass by the way, intelligent too." Jimmy liked his women voluptuous, an accurate description for her.

Astute too, confronted Jean Smith with the photographic

evidence. Even told her they had been led to believe that the deceased liked young children but she didn't flinch. Agreed it was she in the picture but it was innocent. Said "she remembered the incident well, her father had to swat a bee in the bedroom, she was terrified of them." Sounded like she had been told what to say to Adams.

"Julie seemed to think that she had the explanation ready for such an occasion, too pat for her liking. She still maintained that they had a normal family upbringing."

The real reason Jimmy called was that he had managed to delve into more of William Smith's private life, not the life that they had been given to understand.

According to his preacher, William was a 'gift' from God. Became their Church Warden, a position the preacher had trouble filling on account of the unsociable hours. The Youth Club often left a mess: William would always turn up before the end to help clean up.

"Did the preacher say when William became a born again con artist?" Jimmy looked at his cynical friend.

"Apparently, his conversion was quite recent. Perhaps when his beloved Elsie passed away." More likely Elsie was no longer around to rein in his appetites. Jimmy ran through the notes he had made on William Smith. Had been a traveller before the family qualified for social housing. Jean, the daughter, became pregnant at thirteen years old. The mother claimed it was another traveller but they had their suspicions it was the father. The police often visited thanks to young Freddie's thieving. He seemed to be the only family member who came to their attention.

Fifteen years ago, William Smith was prosecuted by the DSS for claiming invalidity benefits. A chronic back problem stopped him from finding gainful employment. But, he was found to be working in the black economy, going across to France to bring back cigarettes and alcohol. When stopped, he claimed it was for personal consumption. He gave up whom he was working for in exchange for community service. Possible motive.

"All this I already knew. I've read the reports too." Jimmy told him to have a little patience he was coming to the best bit.

"Jolenta Bolenza, the polish cleaner." Adams nodded, not a name or figure easy to forget. Jimmy explained that after her interview at the station, she had walked into the migrant workers drop-in centre attached to St Martins and requested help. She was frightened if she told her story she would be sent back. The aid organization arranged for her to see the duty immigration advisor.

She was in the UK on a holiday visa and shouldn't be working but had run out of money. A friend arranged work with the Primary Care Agency. Her first day on the ward and that horrible man wanted her to do things to him in the bathroom. She was frightened. He said he knew people who could make her disappear. He knew where the bodies were buried, she would never be found again.

Maciej knew, she told him. He said he would sort it out, make it go away. Then they heard the man was dead. Maciej Waclaw was an important person in her community but she was even more frightened of him than the horrible man. Adams made a note to re-interview the cleaner.

He told Jimmy of his concerns. The investigation was dragging on. Fisher threatened to cut the team by half, if there was no significant break through by the end of the week. This was going to be Adams' last chance for Detective Inspector. If he got this one wrong, he would be lucky to stay in CID.

The next few hours went by in a haze of alcohol. Jimmy Benton recalling the old days when Jonathan was an eager constable. Even then he was a pain in the backside.

The session with Jimmy had gone on late into the night. The notes he had scribbled were now a crumpled mess underneath him. His head and body ached, he felt as if he had been rolling around inside a washing machine. The pain in his back was caused by Jimmy Benton's worn out settee, vaguely remembered Jimmy saying goodnight, but very little else.

He needed a shower and a shave. His mouth felt as though he had grown fur inside it. He needed clean clothes and a suit he had not slept in. After scribbling a note for Jimmy, he collected his papers and crept out.

Chapter 13

Leaving his clothes in a crumpled heap on the landing he got straight into the shower. The hot water eased his aching muscles. Too old to be kipping down on sofas. Still it was a good night, apart from the Doreen thing that is. Him and Jimmy covered a lot of ground on the investigation, he knew more now where he was going.

On arriving back at the station he headed straight for the canteen. Within minutes, his full English arrived. The canteen staff always made sure he was looked after. It was Adams who led the protest against closure of the canteen and the staff looked upon him as the saviour of their employment.

Jake sneaked out early, careful not to wake his partner. The evening had been a resounding success even though he was late home. They shared a few details of the investigation. It seemed to turn his partner on and the sex had been amazing. He knew if his partner had been awake when he left their apartment they would still be making love right now.

Heading down to the canteen, desperate for a bacon sarnie, wondering if Adams would still be in a grumpy mood. Bacon, being a high cholesterol food, was banned at home. He missed it dreadfully, always ordered when he arrived early for work. It was the only secret he kept.

"Jake, just the man. No time for any breakfast, we're off to the cleaning company. With any luck, we'll catch them still there." He didn't even bother to take off his jacket.

Adams explained the need to speak once again to Maciej Waclaw. They arrived before the office had opened and waited in the car. See thought Jake, I did have time for a bacon sarnie after all.

A brand new black BMW pulled up behind them. They both got out of the car as the woman driver stepped out of her vehicle. She smiled at the two men. Jake looked surprised but smiled back, went over and kissed her on both cheeks.

Adams coughed and looked pointedly at Jake waiting to

be introduced to this rather beautiful woman.

"Sir, may I introduce Christine Mortimer, the owner of this establishment. I just didn't make the connection."

"A relation, I'm guessing."

"My mother sir, well actually my stepmother." Christine Mortimer smiled at Adams. He beamed back, looking her up and down appreciatively. In that moment, she knew he was hers for the taking.

He explained they needed to speak to one of the employees again. She looked at him in surprise, said she had no idea what had been going on. Coyly she smiled at Adams. Jake recognized the look, seen her at dinner parties disarming the male guests.

Looking across at Jake he muttered that he would speak to him later. She invited them in and made them coffee, began to flirt outrageously with Jonathan.

"Please don't be too hard on Jake, he'd really no idea I own this company. My father left it to me. When Jake's father was very ill, I put in a manager who has been first class, I rarely need to visit.

"So why are you here now?"

He liked the way she crossed her legs, smoothed down her skirt.

Christine Mortimer explained that the VAT return was due and she always checked that it was correct, didn't want to break the law, let Jake down, now did she.

Jonathan wondered what it would be like to kiss those luscious lips. Nestle between those breasts. He knew he was staring but didn't care.

The flirting was interrupted by the arrival of the Office Manager. Adams went out to meet her. As instructed by him, she had collected Maciej Waclaw at the end of his shift.

"I don't appreciate being rung at home late in the evening. I do have a private life." I bet you do Adams thought.

Maciej Waclaw looked alarmed when he realised the meeting was to be with the police. The Office Manager was about to have another angry outburst when she saw Christine emerging from the back office.

"Kirsty, I'm sure you will appreciate these police officer's have a difficult job. I expect every consideration to be given to them, do you understand?" She nodded and mumbled an apology.

Christine smiled at Jake, kissed him goodbye and proffered her hand to Adams.

"Please, my office and staff are at your disposal. I hope we meet again soon." Adams offered to walk her out to her car. He carried out the ledgers she had come to collect.

"So will Jake be taken off the case? Being a detective is all he has ever wanted to do. He genuinely had no idea that this was my business. He only moved in with us at the end to help nurse his father. By that time, I had already handed over day to day running to a manager." He held open the car door. She wound down the window and he leaned in to speak to her. Her perfume filled his senses.

"I'm sure something can be sorted out. Perhaps we can discuss it over dinner."

She smiled.

"How about I cook you a meal this evening?" Jonathan jotted down the address and waved as she drove away.

Christine did know that they were coming to interview Maciej Waclaw; Kirsty had rung to complain about Adams calling her. Christine had promised she would have words with them, the reason she had turned up this morning.

Maciej Waclaw claimed he could not understand their questions. His English was very bad. Adams knew better, suggested to him they might as well take him into custody, charge him with the murder of William Smith, sort out an interpreter later.

"Murder, I no murder." He looked around for an escape route, became agitated, shouting in his own language. Adams didn't speak Polish but knew he wasn't being sociable. Jake gestured the cleaner put his hands out, then cuffed him. He would be going with them to the station for further questioning.

The short journey seemed to have helped his understanding of the English language considerably; apparently the Polish police were keen to have him back.

He would co-operate, sort out the misunderstanding, no need to involve the Polish police. They told him they knew Jolenta had talked to him about William Smith. Did he tackle the victim, kill William Smith for revenge?

Waclaw roared with laughter. He cared nothing for the girl. He just saw it as a chance to make some money. Blackmail him. Why would he want him dead? Smith was worth more to him alive, at least until he had told him everything. Adams asked about the alcohol found in the deceased bedside cabinet. Waclaw admitted he gave it to him, as a sign of good faith.

"She's very young to be your stepmother. Close are you?" Adams just came right out with it. He had been racking his brains as to how he could bring the subject up but what the hell, just come out with it.

"Christine was good to me when my father died. I'm estranged from my own mother."

"Why?"

"It's personal sir, has no bearing on my job or the investigation. Am I still part of the investigation sir? I swear to you, I really had no idea Christine owned the company."

"I don't think anyone from the agency is involved in the death. The governor is thinking of cutting my team, I can't afford to lose another officer."

"Thank you sir, I won't let you down."

"For the time being, this information must be only between you and me. Do you understand?" Jake nodded.

Chapter 14

Jonathan Adams had been willing the day to go quickly. Now he wished he had more time to make a decision. He had tried on a number of outfits. Would she be expecting formal or casual? Didn't want to look too laid back but not too formal either. With Doreen, it was what he had been wearing to work that day. He rarely made an effort for Doreen, perhaps that was why they drifted apart. But Christine well she was different. More sophisticated. He showered and put on clean underwear.

Unsure, red or white, he had purchased both. The flowers, were they too ostentatious? Perhaps he should have got the chocolates after all. It was as though he were going on his very first date, hoped it wouldn't be the same though. Then he had too much Dutch courage and threw up all down her kaftan.

He knocked. Classy was the word that came to mind. He stuttered, his first date all over again.

"What do you prefer to be called? Jon or Jonathan?" She ran her tongue over her lips and along the line of her teeth, a sensuous mouth.

He wanted her to call him darling but said Jonathan would do. He had been discreet, as she requested. Not mentioned to Jake that they were meeting for dinner.

She asked him about his job. Did he enjoy being a detective? He said he did. He asked her about her former husband, Jacob Mortimer. What was he like? Their paths had never crossed. Jacob had been her soul mate, no secrets. He asked why Jacob Mortimer had taken early retirement, went into private investigations. Christine told him about the break up of his marriage, how they found one another, explaining that when he was ill, Jake came onto the scene. Jake, the son she never had. Adams didn't want to talk about father and son anymore. He wanted to talk about her, asked about her family.

"My parents died together in a car crash."

"No brothers or sisters?"

"My parents were quite old when I was born. They had almost given up the idea of having a child. I was their special gift my father always told me."

"So that's how you met Jake's father then?" Christine shook her head.

"I met Jacob through a friend of my father's, Andrew Giles. He was the family solicitor, thought Jacob and I, we might get on, even though he was much older than me."

"Is he still your solicitor?"

"Yes, why?"

"Nothing, the name has come up recently that's all."

He didn't know why, just blurted it out. Asked if she knew a William Smith. She thought for a moment, couldn't recall but Jake may have mentioned the name. She stifled a yawn.

"Sorry, it really has been a very long day. When a woman gets to my age she needs all the beauty sleep she can get."

He could not imagine her looking more beautiful and sexy than she did at this very moment but he reluctantly took the hint. Thanked her for a wonderful evening and hoped they could do it again. She said she would like that very much.

The goodbyes, Adams always found awkward. Did he kiss her, shake her hand or what? Christine stood on tiptoe and lightly brushed his lips with a kiss. He stepped back fearing the stirring in his loins would make contact and embarrass him. He would have lingered but for the beep on the horn of his ordered taxi. She waved as he got in, blowing him a kiss as they drove away. He had taken the bait, now to carefully reel him in.

There had been much about the investigation Christine wanted to ask him. Michael had cautioned her to take things slowly. That was fine with her, she had been waiting all her life to become involved with her real family and she wasn't about to lose any of them to prison, particularly as somebody else had committed the murder. Besides, he was putty in her hands.

When he arrived back home, Adams had fully intended to do some work on the reports for the governor. He had no illusions about staying the night on the first date. Classy ladies like Christine, well you had to let them make the first move. He imagined she would want to be in control of the situation. He so wanted her to be in control of him. God did he want to see her again. He had noticed that when she crossed her legs, he could just see the outline of her suspenders. Her breasts were doing their best to escape from the prison of her buttoned up silk blouse. She had kicked her shoes off and he could see the crimson toe nails through the fine black stockings.

Cocoa and late night radio, listening to all the sad people calling in, that usually did the trick. His head hit the pillow and he was asleep within minutes. Had been determined to dream of him and Christine together, lying in a scented bath, candles all around. Just as he leaned forward to cup a breast, the face of William Smith appeared. He woke with a start, his erection quickly deflating.

*****

Jake knew he was later than promised. The flower seller had already packed up and gone home, he would have to wing this one. His partner had prepared their special meal, opened a bottle of wine and had been looking forward to one of their loving evenings. He knew by the flouncing around in the kitchen, he was in for an argument.

"Your job, your bloody job always comes before me, us. Adams treats you like shit, the money is lousy and still your job comes before me!" Jake tried his little boy lost look but it was beyond that.

"You keep me shut out. I'm not even allowed to share your day. I tell you about mine."

Jake tiptoed into the kitchen and put his arms around the slim body with the perfect bum.

"I'm really sorry. You smell delicious. Let's skip dinner

and go straight to bed."

"The meal is ruined."

"I'll have to devour you instead." An arm came up to caress the back of his neck. Jake grabbed the hand and began sucking on the fingers, savouring the taste, olives and garlic. No matter what they argued about, they always made up with mind-blowing sex; it just got better every time.

Jake closed his eyes and let out a deep sigh. His nipple was being rolled between two fingers, the stirring in his loins starting all over again.

"So, has the Neanderthal any clue who the killer is?" With that one sentence, everything changed for Jake.

"I'm sorry it's never happened to me before."

"It's okay, perhaps you're just not in the mood, it's no big deal. We can just lay here and have a cuddle."

"I'm always in the mood with you. It's Adams. I keep seeing his face with that stupid grin plastered across it."

"What's he done now?"

"Nothing. It's what he might do. I think he has the hots for Christine."

"You're joking, she has better taste that that." Jake explained how they had met at the cleaning company. He saw the look in Adams' eyes. The same look he had when their eyes met.

"What if they become very serious, he could even, God forbid, become my step-step father."

"I shouldn't think that very likely. From what I know of Christine, I think her tastes are much more refined than a plod." Jake grabbed a pillow.

"I'm a lowly plod too you know."

"Yes but I like a bit of rough."

Chapter 15

He slept in late, always did when he had a broken night. Drove the car to the newsagents, just couldn't be bothered to walk.

What possessed him to ask Christine Mortimer about William Smith? But he knew why, Andrew Giles.

"Good morning Mr Adams and how are you today?"

"Very well, Mr Patel and yourself?"

"I too am well, since you spoke to those young men, I have no more trouble. Only the very young ones, take the sweets. They think I don't know. But Ms Smith, she is very good. Her boys, they are the biggest culprits. I tell her what they take and she pays me."

"Are we talking about Shirley Smith, Mr Patel?"

"No, her mother, Jean, very nice lady, hardworking, had a hard life you know."

"No, I don't know, help me out here."

"Well, I am not one to gossip but Jean, well she help my wife when she was ill, unable to look after our house properly. She tells my wife about her dreadful father. He beat her you know, made her do things."

Adams stood to one side as Mr Patel served the queue that had built up behind him.

"Mr Patel, can I ask how did you get to know Jean Smith?"

"She came in with her daughter and the boys. Saw the card in the window asking for help with light housework. She was a hard worker.

"The boy's father, Wayne I think he is called, he came round one day and said she wouldn't be coming back. Not a nice person at all. Said, none of their women were going to work for the likes of me.

"She came around the next day, very embarrassed and apologetic, spoke to my wife, told her about the men in her family. Her father and her brother."

"Mr Patel, would you and your wife be prepared to make a statement if it is needed?"

"But of course, you help us with those boys, we will help you back."

Adams thanked the newsagent, paid for his newspapers and returned home.

The day was turning out sunny and warm. Spur of the moment he decided on a trip to the seaside, hadn't heard anything from Dave Spencer for a few days. He decided not to ask Christine to join him on the trip. Christine was more Bournemouth than Leysdown on Sea.

He thought about ringing Jake but he had made it very clear to him when he wasn't shifted in, his weekends were his private personal time. Adams was convinced he was seeing a married woman.

He rang Jimmy Benton asked him if he fancied some jellied eels and a kiss me quick hat. Best offer he'd had all week he said. Adams arranged to pick him up at midday. Jimmy Benton was already outside waiting.

"You're eager."

"Not really, I have to constantly check and recheck, sometimes it takes me half an hour to leave the house."

"That's what made you such a good copper, your attention to every detail. We were all surprised when you turned in your papers."

"Couldn't stand the scum walking and then when I was accused of excessive force, you know the drunk driver case, killed the little girl in her pushchair."

"I remember, got off on a technicality."

"That's the one, technically smashed his head on the side of my police car. I had the choice, resign and keep my pension, or be suspended and take a chance on losing everything. He got away with murder, he wasn't going to get away with my bloody pension as well."

"Didn't he get killed in a hit and run a few months later?"

"Remorse is a strange emotion. He got drunk and walked

out in front of a car. I heard he couldn't live with the guilt of it and that's all I'm prepared to say on the subject." Adams knew better that to probe further.

He asked Jimmy if he was able to make a decent living out of his private work. Jimmy confessed he was so busy he had to turn away work. Never turned away the sort of work Jonathan gave him though, kept him in touch with old friends. Needed a partner really, with experience, used to be on the job too.

"I'm not ready to give up just yet, but thanks for the offer. It was an offer?"

Jimmy nodded and asked why exactly they were travelling down to Kent.

Adams explained the tenuous connection between George Parker and William Smith. Parker was killed on the island. Freddie Smith was staying at Her Majesty's pleasure there. He didn't like coincidence, didn't believe in it.

"Do you think that George Parker killed William Smith and went down to collect from Freddie?"

"Possibly, but he didn't have anything to give him as far as we know."

"Unless of course we're talking information. William Smith well he'd been around. Could have picked up some information. Wouldn't surprise me if he'd been an informant at some stage." That train of thought had not occurred to Adams, he knew getting Jimmy on board had been the right thing to do.

"Jimmy, did you have any dealings with a Jacob Mortimer, used to be on the job, went freelance like yourself?"

"Jake's old man you mean? Interested in the widow Christine are we?" Adams hoped he hadn't blushed.

"I only met the woman for a moment Jimmy, I just wondered if your paths had ever crossed."

"He was north London, always been south London myself. Met him once at a leaving do. Seemed a nice chap. Far too old for the fragrant Christine."

"You met her too?"

"Yup they'd not been together long. Very keen to show her off as I recall. He wasn't what you would call charismatic, ugly bugger really. I think he just wanted to let the rest of us know he could pull a classy woman like her. She wasn't too impressed by the rest of us though. I think that was one of the reasons he went freelance."

"She told me Andrew Giles her family solicitor had introduced them. He was already working freelance when they were introduced. Did some work for her, checking out a business rival."

"Lot of conversation from only meeting a moment." Jimmy grinned.

"Yes all right, I went for a meal at her place but for Christ's sake keep it to yourself."

"Did you pull?"

"I will not dignify that remark with an answer."

"I'll take that as a no then."

Chapter 16

Adams reached the top first but only just. Not as fit as he thought he was. It was an isolated part of the island. The yellow police tape was fluttering in the wind. The sign asking walkers if they had been in the vicinity at the time had fallen over and lay flat on the ground. He propped it up again with the sandbag.

Jimmy came puffing up the hill to join him. The last few yards the pathway narrowed, walking upright became difficult.

Adams asked if he noticed anything unusual.

"I don't think so, nothing much around here, seems to be some sort of nature reserve, rather isolated."

"Just the place to carry out drug dealing or a murder. George Parker's blood was found on a large stone at the edge of the cliff." Adams pointed out the bushes and shrub that obscured a good view of the immediate area.

"George Parker told Wayne he used to live in the area, wanted to see if it had changed much. If he used to live here it must have been in a tent." Adams grinned at Jimmy, his throw away comment pure genius.

"Or an illegal travellers site. William Smith was a traveller, perhaps they knew each other from way back." He scribbled in his notebook, something else to check on Monday morning.

Making their way back down, they collected the car and drove on into Leysdown. Set back off the High Street, Adams found just what he was looking for.

Adams ordered two pints. They found an empty table and waited patiently. If they wanted information about the old days, they best speak to Henry. The barmaid said she would give him the wink when he turned up and thanks very much she would have a gin and tonic for herself.

Henry was a sprightly ninety year old, didn't drink pints he said only double whisky. Adams brought him pie and

91

chips as well. In between mouthfuls he told them about the travellers who used to live on the island. How in the good old days everyone was poor, all working class see, they mostly got on. Not like today, always moved on. Jimmy nodded in agreement.

Adams asked him if he remembered the Smith family of travellers.

"You dense or something, most called Smith. Those that weren't answered to that anyways."

Adams showed the old man a photo of William Smith. He shook his head. "Might have been here." He briefly glanced at the photo of George Parker, returned it to Adams and shook his head. Adams asked if he would look at it again, take his time, Henry was adamant, never seen him before.

"Afternoon gents." Adams looked up to see the smiling face of Dave Spencer. The two pool players who had been smoking something they shouldn't moved towards the rear door but were stopped by the presence of a burly copper.

"I was wondering how long before you arrived." Adams knew they had been observed going onto the island, word would get back.

"Not very sociable, on my patch without letting me know."

Adams feigned surprise at meeting him.

"I'm not working. Just come down for the day." Spencer doubted that very much. Jimmy ordered another pint.

"So you're just down for the day as well?"

Jimmy grinned.

"Only here for the jellied eels and a kiss me quick hat."

"Look Dave, we're not trying to step on anyone's toes. My priority is my murder. There's a connection to the island, not just that Freddie Smith is banged up here."

Jimmy handed Dave Spencer a pint.

Dave Spencer admitted that they had made very little progress in the George Parker murder but he was working along the lines of a robbery gone wrong. Parker had been drinking the evening before his death in the Admiral Nelson,

Blue Town. Blue Town was an area near the docks, rough and ready like the clientele of the Admiral Nelson. It was not an easy pub to find, sited down one of the back streets, so he had to know the area well to find it.

George Parker had been looking to buy dope, a large quantity by all accounts. Knew he would have little trouble buying locally, most of the suppliers are from your way anyhow, Dave Spencer told Adams. They were still harassing the local dealers, as yet none of them admitted to supplying him. Dave seemed to think he probably purchased his dope from more than one person as most of the local dealers didn't keep large amounts, safer that way.

Adams explained he was looking for a connection between William Smith and George Parker as he felt that Freddie Smith was somehow involved, even though he was banged up.

Spencer told him they had received a complaint from a solicitor called Andrew Giles, they were to investigate possible harassment by Adams on Freddie Smith. He advised him to keep a low profile for the time being, not visit the prison or be seen in the vicinity.

"How can a low life like Freddie afford the fees of Andrew Giles?" Jonathan Adams remarked to Jimmy, after Dave Spencer had left them to it.

"Probably gets a family discount."

Henry, the old boy, had told them of trouble caused by the travellers in the summer of 1966 same time as the World Cup. A child went missing on the day we brought home the trophy. His parents blamed the travellers, vigilantes tried to burn down their caravans, a number of people were arrested.

Jimmy said he would look into the incident. William Smith or George Parker might have been involved.

Adams treated Jimmy to his jellied eels but was unable to find a kiss me quick hat. Just as well Jimmy told him, wouldn't want people to get the wrong idea about them.

They travelled back through Sheerness, following the sign for the docks and Blue Town. It took them a while but they managed to locate the Admiral Nelson. It was now an all day open pub. Adams said he fancied an orange juice.

The Admiral Lord Nelson had a reputation in the late fifties, early sixties. A photograph of the Krays and their dear old mum sitting in the pub garden took pride of place over the mantle of the open fire The Krays were standing in the centre, arms around a small woman seated at a wooden table. Either side of them were a number of men, in their Sunday best, caps in their hands, as a sign of respect for Violet Kray.

Had William Smith or George Parker been staying local, they almost certainly would have come to pay their respects to the Krays. To be photographed with the Krays would have been an honour. The publican said they could buy a copy if they were that interested. Sold quite a few to those who came down from London, remembered the old days when the east end used to be full of cockneys not Asians. Might as well make some money out of it. As they drove back to London, a thought occurred to Adams.

"You know one of the Krays preferred young boys!"

Jimmy advised him tread carefully.

Chapter 17

The idea of an involvement by the Krays in his case, both excited and alarmed him. All the older coppers he knew had a tale to tell concerning the Krays.

Christine, he must tell Christine. Bet her old man never had a case involving the Krays. She had told him she found all the old East End villains interesting. Had read quite a bit about them in fact.

While collecting the Sunday papers he had missed a call from her. She wondered if he would be free for lunch today. Would he!

"I'm sorry I missed your call, popped down to the corner shop. Yes I would love to come thank you. I will assume it is around one o'clock and arrive then, unless I hear otherwise." Adams hated leaving a message on her answerphone. Did he sound desperate or needy, probably both. Still, too late now.

He hadn't bothered to have a shave when he got up this morning but quickly rectified the situation. His usual Sunday attire, jogging bottoms and a tattered black police issue tee shirt did not fit the occasion.

She seemed much more relaxed than the last time, or perhaps it was him who was more relaxed. Jonathan told her of his recent visit to the Isle of Sheppey, showed her the copy of the photograph of the Krays. He explained that he thought it possible that one of the young men could well be George Parker or William Smith.

"You mentioned William Smith last time, who is this George Parker?" Christine feigned indifference to her question.

"George Parker is a murder victim but I've a hunch he is connected to William Smith somehow."

Christine asked him about the murder of George Parker, she was sure she hadn't read about it. No you wouldn't have he told her. George Parker was murdered in Kent, the Isle of Sheppey.

Christine knew from her early enquiries that her birth parents had been travellers, following the seasons. They visited Kent frequently for the hop picking. She scrutinized the picture. One of the young men could have been her father. The meal was superb. Jonathan was directed to the armchair while she stacked the dishwasher. She joined him in the sitting room, he was decidedly mellow, would have told her anything.

"So what sort of week have you had?" He knew he should be discreet but she was Jake's stepmother for goodness sake, practically part of the investigation.

Jonathan told her they had ruled her agency out of any involvement with the murder. She leaned forward and lightly touched his arm.

"Thank you."

He couldn't believe the sexual excitement. She touched his arm, held his gaze a moment longer than necessary.

"Do you now have a motive for the murder?" She smiled sweetly at him whilst popping a tot of whisky in his coffee.

"At the moment, motive is still not confirmed. However, I do believe William Smith may have abused his daughter Jean over a long period of time. He planned to move in with her daughter Shirley. Powerful motive wouldn't you say?"

"Do you think that she killed her own father?"

"Not really, but I think she has an idea who might have done. This mysterious brother of hers for instance."

She realised that it was time to implement the second part of their plan.

"I know you're the policeman and the expert." He smiled indulgently accepting her compliment.

"Travellers like William Smith get up to all sorts of things. His death may be to do with criminal activities, but what do I know?"

They were interrupted by the sound of the doorbell. Christine excused herself and went to greet her other visitors.

"Jake, what a nice surprise, two policemen in one day. Jonathan and I have just finished lunch."

Jonathan stood as Jake and another man entered the room.

"Sir." Jake nodded to Adams, unsure quite what to do next.

"You must be Jake's boss." He held out his hand in greeting.

"Michael Jones. I'm a friend of Christine. Thought I'd pop over with a bottle. I didn't expect her to have company, two policeman, better watch myself." Jake stared at Michael, the last thing he wanted was for his lover to try and make a fool of his boss, which he thought would not be too difficult.

Michael stood with his arm around Christine, whispered in her ear. She giggled at their little exchange. Adams didn't figure her for the sort of woman who had a toy boy.

Christine went into the kitchen to put on more coffee and Michael plonked himself down in the armchair opposite Jonathan. Jonathan studied him closely.

"Close friend of Christine's then?" Jonathan queried.

"Yes very, I comforted her when her husband died. Much too old for her really, needed someone young to keep her happy, if you get my meaning." Michael was really enjoying himself.

"Christine told me she went off the rails a little when her husband died, said she did some really stupid things but she's over it now, looking for sophistication in a relationship these days." Jake grinned, one nil to the boss. But Michael wasn't to be outdone.

"Does she still do that thing with the chocolate fingers?" He grinned up at Jake.

"Sorry it took so long everyone. I'm afraid I seem to have no more scones left but I've found a packet of chocolate fingers if anyone wants any."

"Sorry darling, I really can't stay. Jonathan, nice to meet you. Take care." Christine followed Michael out to the front door. He kissed her and whispered what had occurred in the sitting room. She slapped him on the arm.

"Sir. Take no notice. He was only trying to wind you up.

Christine wouldn't look twice at him."

"Course she wouldn't anyway, not his type. His type, don't sleep with women. Homosexual."

Christine glided back into the room, winked at Jake.

Jake quickly gulped down his coffee, said he couldn't stay long, had only popped in to see if she needed anything doing.

Jake stood to leave, told Christine to stay where she was, he would see himself out.

Christine smiled at Jonathan. Gestured for him to join her on the sofa.

"Now where were we?"

Michael was sitting in his car just around the corner. Jake jumped in absolutely furious with him.

Michael leaned across and kissed him gently on the lips.

"I needed to meet him. You spend so much time together, I was beginning to wonder if you fancied him more than me." Jake laughed. He never could stay angry with Michael long.

"He knew you were gay anyway, said so. Christ if he ever found out, I'd never get to work in his team."

Jonathan moved in closer. He was out of practice. With Doreen he never bothered much with foreplay, she never seemed to like it much. He could feel a stirring in his loins, hoped Christine wouldn't notice. A gentle stirring in his trousers, he still had what it takes! His mobile. He fumbled in his pockets, couldn't remember where it was.

"Damnation, bloody thing!"

"This had better be good, I'm not on call."

Chapter 18

The Driscolls were giving him major grief. They ran the prison, nothing was done without their say so. The death of their drug supplier was causing them problems. They seemed to think he knew something about it, what with his recent visits from the filth.

He needed to get out now, even though he only had four days before his parole application, needed to buy himself time away from the Driscolls.

He had been feigning appendicitis. But the governor had arranged for him to see the visiting doctor, not allowed him out to the hospital. The only other option was segregation in the sex offenders' wing but the thought made his skin crawl.

The bastard Adams could get him out early, take him back to London to assist with further enquiries. He would need to give him something worthwhile. Unfortunately, the hold he had over his old man was also a hold over a more powerful individual.

*****

Jonathan Adams could not believe he had missed out on sex with Christine Mortimer. He would have been a fantastic lover, so much so she would be begging him for more but no. When he came to it, he had the choice of Christine or a motive for William Smith's murder. He would have chosen Christine but she insisted she would still be waiting when he returned, indeed looked forward to hearing of his adventures in Kent as she put it.

"I'll be waiting, no matter how late." That's what she said to him as she gave him a lingering deep kiss on her doorstep.

Jake who was already waiting in the police car looked away embarrassed. He had been in a secluded lay by with Michael when his mobile had vibrated. Michael liked outdoor sex; the excitement of being caught really turned him on. Turned Jake on too but he had more to lose.

"I can't believe I'm doing this. Have you any idea what I have just turned down."

Jake was clearly embarrassed, did not want to know.

"Too much information sir. Have we any idea what Freddie Smith has?"

"He better be giving up the killer of his old man and the whereabouts of Lord Lucan."

Their driver had been instructed to take them as far as Clacketts Lane Services. The Kent Police would take them from there. Detective Inspector Dave Spencer would be waiting for them with a driver.

At Clacketts, Dave and his driver were waiting in an unmarked car. Detective Chief Superintendent Arthur Fisher, Adams' boss, had as a matter of courtesy informed Kent Police of their impending visit. Dave Spencer was curious, maybe they could furnish him with more information regarding his own murder investigation.

The interview was to take place at Sittingbourne Police Station. Freddie had been adamant he would disclose no information whilst still at the prison. Dave Spencer agreed he would stay in the viewing room providing Adams pressed Freddie on information on the murder of George Parker.

Driving down the motorway, Dave Spencer brought Adams and Jake up to speed with his investigation.

George Parker had purchased drugs from a number of dealers on the island. Dave Spencer wanted Adams to interrogate Freddie concerning this. Parker was found with neither drugs nor money in his possession. It was important they find out if the drugs ever reached the prison.

Adams and Jake entered the interrogation room. Freddie looked agitated and rather unnerved.

"I'm not talking until the screw is gone." Adams nodded to the Prison Officer who had accompanied Freddie from the Island. His orders had been to remain with the prisoner at all times. However Adams pulled rank, told him there was a nice canteen, go get himself something.

Freddie visibly relaxed when left with just Adams and Jake.

"So Freddie, what exactly is so important that it interrupts my social life?"

"I have information concerning a disappearance but I need some guarantees."

"There was me thinking you wanted to do your civic duty."

"George Parker. Did the drugs reach the buyers before he sang soprano?" The question threw Freddie for a brief moment. His surprise not lost on Dave Spencer watching intently in the viewing room.

"I'm only talking about the information I have on the disappearance."

"Fine, but will the Driscolls believe that?"

Freddie blanched; perhaps a beating by the Driscolls was the better option after all. He requested a cup of coffee and a cigarette. Said he needed to go to the toilet. Jake was assigned to accompany him. Adams and Jake knew it was just a delaying tactic but let him have his way. One of the constables pointed them in the right direction. Jake checked the cubicle first, no window. He waited right outside, said he would give him no more than two minutes.

Freddie flushed the toilet. Whilst washing his hands, he caught Jake's reflection in the mirror.

"Does that bastard Adams know you're a poof then?" Jake chose to ignore the question.

"I can always tell you know."

"If you're finished we'll get back. We can't keep you too long. I'm sure you're being missed on the island already." Jake smiled, Freddie's smirk quickly disappearing.

As they re-entered the interview room, Adams had placed a second coffee and a pack of cigarettes in front of him.

Freddie set out his terms; the next four days in their station nick. He would not go back to the prison. Adams set out his terms. Tell him what he knew and he would decide if it was worth it.

"Do you think I'm that thick?" Yes Adams told him he did.

"Freddie people disappear all the time. We also know that your old man was a paedophile, liked very young girls. Understand you were partial to them as well. Unless you've got more to give me then I think we're done here." Adams nudged Jake and they both stood to leave.

"There is a Detective Inspector Spencer, wants to talk to you about George Parker. We'll leave you to it. Remember me to Danny Driscoll, me and him go way back."

As arranged, they went directly to the viewing room where Dave Spencer was waiting. Adams wanted to observe Freddie whilst he was left to his own devices.

"When you mentioned George Parker, his body language changed. I was watching closely through the mirror. He definitely knows something." Adams had to agree with him.

All three detectives retired to the canteen.

"Sir you don't think that William Smith could be another Fred West?" Jake voiced what Adams was thinking.

"Hope not. Still don't think they accounted for all the bodies there." Adams glanced at his watch. Told Dave Spencer he would give Freddie another fifteen minutes to think about his options. Just to add to Freddie's stress, Adams had deliberately removed the packet of cigarettes when they left the room.

It didn't take long. Freddie had already decided how much he would need to secure his terms but had wanted to test how little he could get away with revealing.

He gave up the body and little else.

Chapter 19

Freddie demanded he be put in a safe house. Powerful people had been involved. He would not feel safe in jail.

It took until late Sunday evening for arrangements to be made. The information supplied by Freddie Smith was way over a Detective Sergeant's head. Adams was required to call Detective Chief Superintendent Fisher at his home, not recommended if you wish to keep both testicles attached to your body.

Adams had refused to make any arrangements until he had more information.

Monique Cecile. All he needed to say.

Monique had been eighteen years old, coming over to England by ferry. Arrangements had been made for her to work as an au pair for the summer, improve her English. She never arrived, was reported missing by her parents and the Roberts family a few days later. The Roberts had assumed she had changed her mind and her parents thought she was too preoccupied to telephone to say she arrived safely.

Records show that she had boarded the cross channel boat but never left. Twenty-seven years her anguished family had been waiting for news. Her father died a broken man but her mother was determined not to leave this world until Monique had been laid to rest. Well he Freddie Smith could give her the peace of mind she craved.

Adams remembered the case. It hadn't quite made the front pages. The case caught his attention. He had just left school, awaiting his exam results, needed them before he could apply to join the force.

At this stage, it was decided not to contact the Cecile family, raise false hopes. It irked Adams that Freddie was being treated with such deference but he had no choice. He and Jake had been assigned to stay with him at the safe house.

To Adams' surprise, all Freddie's demands were met.

Because of the sensitivity of the operation, they went directly to the two bedroom mansion block flat in South London. They had to make do with the clothes they were wearing. Freddie boy was given a change out of prison issue.

"I don't know about you Jake but this is not how I envisaged spending my Sunday evening." Jake nodded, thinking of the double bed at home.

The intercom system buzzed. Adams and Jake looked at one another. They looked out of the front window. Directly below stood a motorcyclist carrying a large pizza box. Adams dialled direct to the unmarked car sat at a safe distance down the road.

The pizza delivery man was shocked and surprised when pushed up against the wall of the building. The pizza was for them. It had been paid for in cash at one of their smaller outlets. His instructions were to deliver it with the message to enjoy it while you can. Adams decided not to pass on the message to Freddie, told him that it was the wrong address but they would have it anyway.

With Freddie safely tucked up in bed watching the Fantasy Channel, Adams discussed with Jake who could have sent the pizza. The problem as Adams saw it was that only a select few knew which safe house they were using.

Freddie always preferred the dark. His old man often said he could see what he was thinking. Couldn't see so well in the dark. He had been unnerved by the pizza man. Needed to know who sent the message they took great pains for him not to know about. If it was the Driscolls, he needed to let them know they had nothing to fear. Their lucrative industry inside the prison was safe with him.

No what concerned him more was that perhaps the message had been from the powerful individual his old man had been fleecing these past years. It had taken some time for him to get the full story from him and then only because he had got him drunk.

It was on one of his jaunts down to the Kent paedophile group. Freddie had been bigger then, determined they would not take him again. That was when the old man threatened him. He would be buried right there along with the girl from the ferry.

William Smith caught sight of the youth at the Old Bailey, whilst waiting for the case of a friend to start. He was much older now, had filled out his gangly frame but without doubt the killer of Monique Cecile. Jotting down his details, he took no time in contacting him. Of course he denied it, William sent a copy of his video. The killer agreed to pay him regular amounts.

His old man had refused to divulge the name. Freddie would only know when his old man was no longer around to collect his dues. The name would be passed down father to son, a sort of inheritance.

This was the reason that Freddie had been named as next of kin. William Smith's solicitor held a key to a safe deposit box, which held the incriminating video.

What he did know however was that the killer was a very important man within the Metropolitan Police Authority. This is what worried Freddie. Powerful enough to have easily found out where he had been taken. William had assured his son that this person had no idea who he was but he could have been mistaken.

Agreement had been reached by those much higher up the food chain than Adams that Freddie Smith would be kept in the Met's protective custody for the next four days, after which, he would be free to go. Fisher wasn't happy about it either but he was due out. Adams had argued that withholding information on the whereabouts of a body should get him more time but he was overruled. His help in bringing closure to the Cecile family was more important than giving Freddie Smith extra time.

The morning was wet and blustery. Freddie had demanded a full English breakfast. Adams told him to make do with burnt toast; they would stop on the way to wherever they were going.

Clacketts Lane Service Station. Adams was beginning to

feel it was his second home. The assistant behind the counter greeted him like an old friend. He ordered two full English and one vegetarian. The uniformed constable had to make do with a Mars bar. Jake who until quite recently would have been that constable sitting outside, sent out coffee for him.

Freddie knew exactly where the body had been buried but didn't trust Adams. He was determined to hang out the search for as long as possible, four days to be exact. He was pleased he got the assurance of not being sent back to Stanford Hill Open prison. The Driscolls could stitch him up. The idea of a long stretch for murder did not appeal to him.

It suddenly dawned on Adams that they were driving deeper into the Kent countryside. Adams began reminiscing about his holidays as a young lad in the late 1950s. Leysdown, the Isle of Sheppey. Harts holiday camp, the biggest on the island at that time. In common with other young Londoners, it was the nearest he ever got to the sea. Peanut Len on the corner selling his wares. The sounds of the arcades, the smell of candyfloss. Those were the days.

Freddie took the opportunity to have a good look around the island. The main town of Sheerness with narrow Victorian terraced houses had changed little over the years. He knew that the abuse he suffered here as a young lad occurred on one of the many caravan sites on the outskirts of the town. The exact one he had obliterated from his mind. The docks although not used as much these days was still a working dock, being one of the biggest importers of fresh produce with its state of the art cool stores.

As they drove through Minster, Adams suggested they stop off at Warden Point. Freddie Smith was adamant the burial site was not there; he was edgy, reluctant to walk the path to the cliff edge, but Adams insisted, said the view was spectacular.

Adams went first, followed by Freddie and then Jake. The sign requesting assistance with George Parker's murder had again fallen over. Adams stood it back up.

"This is where a murder took place just under a week ago."

"So, nothing to do with me, I was inside remember. It's windy up here can we go back now?" Adams nodded and they trouped back down to the waiting car.

Within an hour they had covered most of the island. Freddie wasn't too sure. Needed to go away and think about it. A map of the area would be useful too. They drove back into London. Freddie Smith was dropped back at the safe house with another shift of babysitters. Adams and Jake had proper work to do.

Chapter 20

The team were already waiting for them when they got back. They had all heard about the breakthrough in the Monique Cecile case, so much for a need to know basis thought Adams.

He tried to play down his involvement but was secretly thrilled that he might be the one to crack the case and give closure to the Cecile family. Better men than he had been assigned to the original case and got nowhere. A result would do him no harm, may even be the case that makes him up to inspector.

Reluctantly, Detective Chief Superintendent Arthur Fisher put Adams in charge of following any leads on the Cecile case. He had wanted to keep it for himself but Freddie Smith had been adamant, he would only deal with Adams and Jake Mortimer. Still he would be there at the Press Conference, pressing the point of the team effort involved.

Adams would have preferred to hand over the day to day running of the William Smith murder to his second in command but as it was technically Jake, he had no choice but to carry on. He was well aware that he needed to give more focus to Smith's murder. They were now into the third week and the trail was becoming very cold indeed. Had it not been for the Monique Cecile revelations, Adams was sure the boss would have cut his team by now.

Jean Smith had been interviewed again but this time at the station. She had Andrew Giles with her. Try as they might they could not get her to admit to any abuse by her father. What they did get but had not asked for was a signed statement from Sanjeve Patel confirming that Jean Smith was in bed with him at the time of her father's murder; backed up by a further statement from the controller of Ace Taxi Service who had called him out to cover for a sick driver, Jean had answered the call.

It still puzzled Adams how a woman like Jean Smith

could afford the likes of Andrew Giles. WPC Julie Burton suggested that perhaps she and Gill Cole see her unofficially later in the week. Gill was used to dealing with abused women, knew the signs, confident they could draw her out.

Jonathan Adams rang the florist, arranged for flowers to be sent to Christine Mortimer. Should he wait till she received them and 'phone for another date or wait until she contacted him? Unsure, he felt he was seventeen again when he had a crush on the librarian. She must have been all of thirty years old but he had been consumed with guilt for lusting after an older woman.

The technical guys had attempted to enhance the image of the hooded man at the hospital, the powers that be were still deciding if it would be worth their while to put it out on the local news.

Jimmy Benton had been looking more closely into William Smith's background particularly in the early sixties, with relevance to any involvement with George Parker. The photograph of the Krays in the pub gardens on the Isle of Sheppey, he traced back to the *News of the World.* Jimmy had a contact in their archives department who after a few pints, was more than happy to reminisce about the good old days. He had been freelance; quite by chance he was on the island at the same time as the Krays. Took the opportunity that presented itself.

He confirmed that the regulars seen on the periphery of the photo were casual labourers down for the summer work. They came for the cherry and hop picking in the nearby area. The travellers who came for most of the summer months worked at the funfairs on the island.

He remembered there being some trouble between the locals and the casual labourers. Not newsworthy or salacious enough to interest the News of the World but the local paper covered the story; it would be in their archives.

Jimmy Benton gave a brief report.

"In July of 1966, there was an incident when a young boy went missing from the fun fair. He was seen in the company of a fairground worker and a young girl. Witnesses at the time stated the young boy did not seem distressed in any way, in fact, a couple of them assumed they were brother and sister. The man and his daughter were never traced despite extensive publicity at the time. The body of the young boy who had been around the age of five years was never found."

Earlier that morning, he had given Detective Chief Superintendent Arthur Fisher an update of the investigation. Fisher was also of the opinion that more bodies may come to light before they found the killer. In view of the increased body count, he arranged for more officers to join the team. Adams requested the secondment of Gill Cole. Her experience with abused families would be invaluable, beside which, she had already become involved as a favour to them.

Adams was concerned that he may have uncovered a paedophile network. He needed to know if William Smith was a participant or an organizer. Some of the enquiries the team had been making had flagged up the interest of the Child Protection Team. They all closely guarded their territory. Fisher advised he couldn't guarantee that Adams would keep the investigation. Arthur Fisher had been summoned by the Assistant Chief Constable to outline what they had already found. His job and reputation were also on the line. Jonathan Adams and the Assistant Chief Constable had history and the ACC was not prepared for his career to be put in the hands of the maverick Adams. Fisher played down the child abuse angle during the meeting, but they needed a break soon or they would lose it.

With the chance of cracking the Cecile case perhaps that wouldn't be such a bad idea thought Adams. The briefing in the incident room had begun to turn into a free for all, voices raised to be heard.

Adams looked up. Hovering in the doorway of the incident room was a nervous young woman. Woman, she looked about twelve years old to Adams. Jake smiled and beckoned her in.

"Boss this is Paula Rogers. She is in her last year as a

graduate in criminal psychology. Doing some work experience. She's helping us out with the admin. Brilliant on the computer."

"My uncle arranged it," she stuttered.

"I suppose he's the Chief Constable." She smiled sweetly at Adams.

"Yes. How did you guess?" Adams sighed, that was all he needed right now, an enemy in the camp. He held out his hand and she passed over the sheaf of papers.

"Jake, sorry, DC Mortimer asked me to look for anything on HOLMES that William Smith could have been involved in. Don't worry, I have clearance, I worked here last year in the summer. As he was a traveller, I researched different areas in Kent where travellers would have been staying in the early sixties. I then cross-referenced information not only with William Smith but missing persons under the age of ten years, then I cross-referenced..." Adams put up his hand to stop her.

"I think I get the picture. Thank you."

"But," she stuttered standing her ground.

"There's more?"

"I can place William Smith and George Parker together when they were younger."

Adams looked at her in total admiration. Two weeks all it took for a student for heavens sake to make the connection. What did it say for the others on his team? Not even two weeks, she had only been working on the project a few days.

"You're a star. I owe you one. In fact we all owe you one."

Paula beamed with pride, took a bow as Adams began a round of applause.

"But." Adams face fell. Why was there always a but.

"But I can only place Andrew Giles with William Smith and George Parker. I'm afraid I can't find any connection with Jean Smith, apart from her being his client."

111

Chapter 21

"So Freddie, you never said that your old man was a boxer?"

"Never said lots of things you didn't ask me about. First rule, never volunteer information, my old man beat that one into me."

Adams pushed across the table an old photograph. Jimmy Benton had come up trumps with the archives from the Medway Gazette, the local Medway Towns' newspaper and a sister paper the Sheppey Gazette. The management prided themselves on keeping old photographs longer than most national papers, plus the fact they hadn't yet copied all their archived material onto microfiche let alone on to a computer.

William Smith was in the pose of a fairground fighter. Bare knuckles. Not quite the Queensbury rules. The sign beside him stated he would fight anyone, any weight. Prize if they could last three rounds.

Adams then produced another old photograph of the Rochester Casino Club. The photo seemed to have been taken early to mid 1960's judging by the few cars parked outside. Top of the bill was 'King of the Casino' Billy Webb versus Jocko Pett. But it was a supporting bout that Adams pointed out to Freddie. Billy Smith versus 'Nosy' Parker, real name George Parker.

Freddie shrugged.

"So did you ever meet George Parker when you were a young lad?"

"Thought you wanted to talk about Monique Cecile?"

"George Parker. Mates with your old man then?"

"If they was scrapping, what do you think?" Freddie feigned disinterest in the conversation but Adams wasn't fooled.

"You would need to ask my old man that. Oops you can't, he's snuffed it and you're still nowhere near finding out who topped him."

"George liked young boys. Did he like you when you

were a lad?"

"You're sick, you know that?"

"I heard your old man liked both, long as they were young, didn't care if they stood up or sat down to piss."

The plain-clothes baby sitter held Freddie back while Jake stepped in front of Adams. This time he had gone too far. Jake steered him into the small galley kitchen and put the kettle on.

"It wouldn't do to antagonise him too much sir. We need him to find the body of Monique Cecile."

"He's jerking us around I know. Time for plain speaking."

Adams had just about had enough. He needed to know William Smith's perversions, felt they had a bearing on his death. Not only that, he was annoyed that Christine had not replied to his messages.

When they returned to the sitting room Freddie was sitting by the window blowing out smoke.

"Is my old man in the frame for the French bird's murder?"

"You tell me. All points to him at the moment. We can put him on the ferry, the last place of a confirmed sighting. As long as it's cleared up and we have someone in the frame makes no odds to me whether we get the right one or not." Jake stared at Adams unable to believe what he heard.

Freddie was in a dilemma. Although not particularly bright, he had the nous to understand that should his old man be fitted up for the murder of Monique Cecile, then he could say goodbye to the money.

He only needed to hold out for another day and a half. His parole would then kick in and he wouldn't even have to talk to them. He needed to keep them sweet however.

"Time to break the old man's first rule. He didn't do it, knew who did and where the body was buried." Freddie told them the story, leaving out a few facts.

William Smith had been on one of his regular booze cruises. He had also picked up some under the counter videos and video recorders of doubtful origin. The bloke he was working for did not want them left alone in the van, lots of villains about, so he stayed on the car deck. He had been in the right place at the right time.

An argument developed between a young couple, well he assumed they were together. Like him they shouldn't have been on the car deck. They seemed to be arguing, she attacked him, he retaliated, smacked her hard across the face. She fell, hit her head on a bulwark to the side of the emergency exit.

By now, the old man was videoing the proceedings, whilst crouched down in the front of the van. The youth lifted up the girl and placed her in the boot of an old Ford Anglia.

When they disembarked back at Dover, he followed the car as it drove around the Kent countryside, keeping a discreet distance.

"Name Freddie, we need the name of this bloke."

"The bastard never told me, said it was best for my health not to know."

"Sir let's hope there's still some evidence left with the body." Adams looked at Freddie.

"I'm still not convinced there is another person involved. Agreed Monique Cecile was a little older than he liked but perhaps he started with the older ones and worked his way down."

"Tomorrow, no more chasing around Kent. Once I've had a butchers at the map, it'll come back to me."

"It had better."

Again they both had to stay with Freddie Smith. Jake excused himself and rang Michael. When they were apart, they would also have 'phone sex. He was in the bathroom with the shower running, the only room with a lock on the door. Michael was teasing him about sharing a room with Adams, pretended to be jealous of what they might get up to.

*****

She opened the front door, surprised at the visitor standing there.

"I wondered when we would be able to speak privately."

"Your door step is not that private." Stepping back she waved him in. He waited in the sitting room while she prepared coffee.

"Why was he eliminated earlier than planned?"

"Jean asked me the same question. The bastard was taken out but not by us. Frankly I'm quite relieved somebody else did him. At lease Jake hasn't been compromised. Personally, I think we just need to cover any tracks we have already left and be thankful."

"Talking about my Jake, you cannot imagine my shock when he brought you home. You could have warned me. I had no idea you were gay."

"Best to be discreet about your sexuality in my line of work. I'm just grateful you didn't give the game away."

"What tell him his boyfriend is my brother who I've just found after years of searching and oh yes, we are in the middle of plotting a murder."

"Well it's over now."

"For you maybe, but I provided a pass and cleaner's uniform. They are missing, could lead back to me."

"Jake will make sure it doesn't. Anyway, we are in the clear. We didn't kill him."

"Do you have any idea who did? Do we having anything to fear from them?" He shook his head.

"We need information as to how the police are progressing. This is where you and I come in."

Michael had told her not to contact Adams just yet. Play really hard to get, then he would tell her everything.

"Hard to get like you did with Jake?"

Chapter 22

She rarely made eye contact, her brain too slow in the connection. Pure chance it happened. Just a split second in time started a chain of events she was powerless to prevent.

She recognized the eyes, remembered the terror she had last seen in them. The mouth was different though. Then there were sores around the lips and nose from the glue sniffing. He didn't cry or snivel, like the others did that was why she noticed him. He was streetwise, one of the feral children. He knew why he was there. Knew there would be pain but it came with the life style he had chosen. A father in prison, his mother on the game to pay for her next fix, what chance did he have? The drugs and booze they plied him with was little compensation. The pain and degradation made him feel like he was no longer a member of the human race, just a piece of meat with no feelings.

Never been able to have a proper relationship with anyone thanks to those bastards. The sex act would always remind him of pain and degradation. He found it easier not to start a relationship. His mental health deteriorating, he spent his twenties a lonely depressed man.

The rapes he endured had given him long-term health problems too. Damage to his rectum resulted in major surgery, left him in constant pain. The first time he had been hospitalised by the bastards he was only eleven years old, his voice hadn't even broken but they liked that, still had the little boy lost look about him.

Social Services had been involved but he was not a grass, the older boys had put him right about grassing. Placed in care he fared no better. The social workers expected him to do the same for them only the difference was he didn't even get paid in booze or cigarettes. He never knew when it would end. At least with the others, he could escape afterwards, have a few hours on his own. That was the reason he absconded, took to living on the streets. If he had to do it then he wasn't going to do it for free. Life on the streets was hard difficult but at least there he had choices. He could demand payment for his services and occasionally, he got to stay in some nice places.

At first he was ashamed she knew the life he used to lead. Terrified she would tell. Knew he couldn't take the humiliation if it became public knowledge, had worked hard to distance himself from the life he used to lead.

She longed to speak to him but found it difficult to communicate. Having promised many years ago, not to speak, her life depended on her silence. At least that's what Mum always told her as she was growing up.

"People think you're simple they have no expectations for you. It will keep you safe, tell no one any different." She had kept the promise but his need for reassurance and comfort was much greater. She slipped him a note, said she would never tell, even if her life depended on it.

At first it was just a nod of acknowledgement. This progressed to a smile and a good morning.

Sheltered from the outside world, she appeared much younger than her thirty-five years, had a childlike quality that appealed to him. Not in the same way as those bastards would have thought of her though.

Sister Bernadette was his salvation. She found him one freezing night as he lay in the gutter. The drugs they had given him to keep him pliant hadn't worked. He was no use to them when he wouldn't play their game. The van just slowed down and they pushed him out the sliding door. He landed at her feet. She was there, dispensing soup and the love of Jesus. She took him in until his broken leg healed. Nobody bothered him there. He let Jesus into his heart, Sister Bernadette said He would make it better, but it was too late for that. The doctors at the hospital gave him the news he was HIV positive. Any hope of a normal life was gone for him but Sister Bernadette and Jesus did not abandon him. They arranged accommodation and employment. But no matter how hard he tried he would never forgive them for what they did, never even if it meant he would lose the love of Jesus. Some things were just unforgivable.

It took a while but they began to open up to each other. Neither one willing to go to the dark place where they first met until the day Mary told him about the plan. The plan Mickey and Jean discussed so carelessly in her presence.

They thought she didn't understand what they were saying you see. Thought she hadn't been a victim, would not comprehend what they were talking about, but she knew. The plan terrified her. They would be the obvious suspects, could even go to prison. Who would look out for her then?

The idea that they should do her bastard father before the others got to him was hers. But he was a willing participant, even begged her to let him do it.

The plan was already in place. We just made a few adjustments. Mary wanted him to drown, let him feel the terror of water filling his lungs, knowing he had very little time left. Tell him I sent you she said.

She wanted him to know who had arranged his murder. The retard bastard daughter that's who. She was only disappointed she wouldn't actually be there.

Getting in was the easy part. They were used to seeing him hanging around. Taking the card was simple. Stupid woman, so busy talking to her lover the Chief Executive, hanging on his every word, she didn't even notice me. Wouldn't you see, she only saw those who could do something for her. That's why I chose to take her entry card. Kept the money from the purse too. The other cards I destroyed.

Mary said to hand the purse back afterwards. Would look less suspicious and they might not make the connection.

It was easy to slip into the ward. Hope I never end up there. Those nurses couldn't care less about the patients. Snoring away in that little office all cosy like.

I hid in the bathroom. I knew he would come. Would be unable to resist the invitation I had given him. I asked did he remember what we did together, how good it was for him, mentioned his special requirement. He used to like that particular perversion; I knew he couldn't resist. He was already aroused when he came in. I had run the bath. The rest was simple. My note I sent him, he had slipped into his dressing gown pocket that was easily retrieved. I left via the emergency exit. Wearing plastic shoes over my own, I left no trace. Everything went as planned, as they had planned.

I whispered in his ear that Mary sends her regards. Then he went under. He wasn't as strong as I remembered him to be.

"I never realised how easy it would be to kill him, or the pleasure it would give me."

Chapter 23

Gill Cole knew the Abelard Estate well, had grown up in the area. Moved out as soon as she was able. Still couldn't believe she had ended up back working the patch.

They drove slowly past the house in Elouise Gardens. She had used her own car, it would make it less obvious to the neighbours they were police, parking at the far end of the road.

"She is in, just seen the net curtain move." Gill was glad to have WPC Julie Burton with her. Jean Smith would open up more to two females.

Adams had suggested they telephone Giles & Associates Solicitors before leaving. See how long they could talk with Jean Smith before her brief turned up. They were in luck. Andrew Giles was in court that morning. They were due a bit of luck for a change.

"Not many people have it delivered these days." Julie pointed out the two pints left on the doorstep.

"Well I certainly don't. Where I live unless you take it in the moment it's left, the little darlings nick it." Julie laughed, remembering the times her Mum would give one of her brothers the money to pop down the corner shop and they would keep the money and borrow a pint from one of the neighbours. She picked up the two milk bottles; they felt warm.

The doorbell was ignored so Gill Cole knocked loudly on the window. Still they waited but Jean Smith didn't bother letting them in.

"She knows it's us. I expect she's under orders from Andrew Giles not to let us in."

"Then I'll have to huff and puff and blow the house down." Gill Cole rattled the letterbox.

"Come on love. You don't want the neighbours knowing your business." She bent down, lifted the letterbox and looked into the hallway. Letting out an expletive she shouted at Julie.

"Call an ambulance!" As Gill Cole sprinted around the back of the house Julie fumbled in her bag for her mobile phone. Almost dropping the milk bottles she cradled the mobile to her ear. Just as she placed the bottles back on the step, she heard the sound of breaking glass. Bending she looked through the letterbox.

Gill Cole was leaning over the prone body of Jean Smith desperately trying to find a pulse. She rolled her on to her back before opening the front door for Julie.

"Mouth to mouth. Can you do the CPR?" Julie nodded, flinging down her bag as she knelt beside Jean.

The paramedics were quickly on the scene, usually were when the call came from a police officer. They managed to resuscitate but lost her again in the ambulance on the way to hospital. They again managed to get her back but her vital signs were poor. Gill gave Julie instructions not to move away from the house, not to let anyone in unless it was Jonathan Adams.

She told the paramedics she would follow on after she had checked out what medication was in the house. What medication wasn't in the house more to the point. Valium, Prozac, painkillers, and lots more tablets not in labelled bottles. She scooped them all up into an evidence bag and took them with her.

She parked in the ambulance bay area, have to chance a wheel clamp, they needed to know what drugs might have been taken. The A and E staff had already done all they could, now it was up to her but Jean Smith was rapidly slipping into a coma.

*****

Adams and Jake arrived just as Julie Burton was seeing off the local beat patrol.

"Even if you were the bleedin' Chief Constable and Home Secretary, you'll not be allowed in. The only one allowed to pass me is my 'guvnor', miserable looking sod more scary than you two could ever be."

Adams smiled. Yes she'd got the description about right. Game girl, she stood her ground.

"Morning 'Guvnor'." Adams nodded to the two beat bobbies. Put one on the front gate and the other on the back. Jake and Julie followed Adams into the house. Again Julie picked up the two bottles of milk.

"Best put these in the fridge, they've gone warm."

"Sir, wait." Adams and Julie turned to Jake hovering in the doorway.

"Something's not right."

"Course it's not right, silly bitch tried to top herself."

"When we came before, you asked me to make tea for you and Jean Smith. The milk, was in a carton. No milk bottles in the kitchen, she doesn't have milk delivered I'm sure of it." Julie looked aghast at Adams.

"I didn't think."

"Also, when I checked the bathroom before, no drugs to speak of."

Adams was of the same opinion; this was looking less like a suicide attempt by the minute.

"Sir look." The alphabet fridge magnets were arranged in the words 'safe with Jesus'.

"Do we know if she was religious?"

"Lapsed Catholic I think."

"Lapsed or not, she would consider it a mortal sin." Adams took out his mobile and called for a Scenes of Crime team.

"Sir. When we drove by the house, I was sure I saw the net curtain move but now I'm not so certain. She'd been lying on the floor for quite a while the paramedics said, so it couldn't have been her."

Adams held his finger up to his mouth and gestured to Jake that they should check upstairs. Julie stood guard at the bottom, bottle of milk in her hand ready for a fight. Any prints would be hers anyway.

Much to Jake's relief, there was nobody hiding upstairs.

What they did find however was a very dishevelled bedroom, drawers and cupboards open, papers and photographs strewn across the unmade bed.

Outside they could hear shouting. From the window Adams could see a man scuffling with the officer he had left at the front gate.

"Where is she? It's my bloody house. I'll go into my own house and you can't stop me." Adams and Jake arrived at the front door at the same time as Sanjeve Patel.

"A neighbour called, said get back home quick. What's happened?"

Adams led him to their car.

"I'd rather you didn't go in just yet, it may be a crime scene."

"Jean, where is she, what's happened, I need to know and right now."

Adams explained that Jean had been found unconscious between the kitchen and hallway. She appeared to have taken an overdose.

"She don't even like taking asprin. She'd never do that, it's a sin according to her religion."

"I'll arrange for a car to take you to the hospital, but I need to ask you a few questions first. What time did you leave for work this morning?"

"Leave, I've not been home yet. On nights this week, I need to be with her. Christ, has anyone called Shirley, she'll go to pieces, can't manage without her mum!"

"Don't worry that's all in hand."

"The fridge magnets…"

"Sod it. I'm not answering any more questions. If you don't take me to the hospital I'll drive meself."

Adams put him in a squad car. The other questions could wait. He would get Gill Cole to stay at the hospital, speak to the boyfriend and the daughter, see if she could find out more.

They went back into the house, at least now they could have a good look around.

"Use gloves both of you and be careful what you touch."

Before they had a chance to have a good look around the Scenes of Crime team arrived.

Chapter 24

It took all Gill Cole's self restraint not to give the 'gobby' cow a slap. In her face screaming and shouting, so close she could smell the nicotine on her breath.

Wayne grabbed her and pulled her in close but still she was screaming like a banshee.

"It's not her fault love, she's just the messenger." Shirley pushed hard against him.

"Course it's their fault, hounding her, not letting up. I'd have tried to top meself if I had to put up with what me mum has this past week." Gill let her rant and rave, get it out her system. She walked down the corridor to get them all a cup of machine tea. Even though the uniformed woman officer had arrived, Adams wanted her to stay, interview any relatives who turned up, in particular the missing brother.

Fearful of the disruption the senior nurse arranged a quiet room for Gill to speak to the distraught Shirley. Gill Cole sat opposite her out of arms reach. Handed over her peace offering of a mug of revolting tea.

Wayne had to get back to the kids. A neighbour was looking out for them but she was going to bingo so he had to rush back. Gill assured him that she would make sure Shirley got home.

"I'm going nowhere while me mum's in here." With a cup of tea and a box of tissues, Shirley began to calm down, to get herself together. The ICU ward allowed one visitor per bed. Sanjeve was sitting with Jean for the moment.

"Sorry about earlier, it's just that me and mum, well we fell out a few days ago over nothing really and now we might not be able to make up." Gill smiled at her anxious tear stained face, said she understood.

"Shirley love, she's holding her own. I get the impression your mum has been through a lot over the years, she's tough."

"She just wouldn't top herself. Even if we weren't

speaking, she would never leave my kids, never."

"So what did you and your mum fall out about then? Me and my old mum were always falling out, usually over boyfriends and staying out late."

"Me granddad. Wayne had taken to meeting him up the pub when he was supposed to be home looking after the kids. He took the kids with him, they played on the bouncy castle in the garden, loved it. But mum just went mental, said the pub wasn't the right place for the boys, said she would have them if Wayne couldn't be bothered to look after them while I was at me bingo."

"So did you usually go with the neighbour who's looking after the boys at the moment?"

"Yes, it's my only bit of pleasure. Mum used to give me the money to go but when we fell out she didn't give it to me but said it was going into an account for the boys."

"Did you see much of your nan and granddad when you were growing up?"

"Not much, me mum and nan didn't really get on and she couldn't even bear to be in the same room as granddad Bill."

"Have you any idea why?"

"She wouldn't say. Once when I had a big win on the bingo, she got tipsy and said I didn't know how lucky I was that I didn't have to cope with what she did."

"Didn't you ask her what she meant?"

"Nah, she's was always saying she had a lousy childhood when she'd had a few."

"Your Uncle. Does he know your mum's here in hospital?"

"Oh my god! Uncle Mickey. He'll go ape when he finds out."

"Do you have a number or an address? I'll have an officer go and collect him, bring him straight here."

"I don't even know if he's in the country. Travels a lot. Only mum knows the number, it's in her head, she always said it was safer that way."

"What about your other Uncle!"

"He's banged up, she wouldn't want him around anyway. They fell out ages ago over Mary."

"Would you like Mary to be here with you?"

"No, she'd only get in the way. Could you stay a bit longer?"

"Sure, why don't I go and get us another drink and something to eat."

"Thanks that would be good. Didn't get a chance to have breakfast."

Gill nodded to the staff nurse as they passed in the corridor. She had a few minutes time for a quick smoke and check for any messages.

She had quite a few, most of them from Jonathan Adams. It seemed that Jean Smith's suicide attempt was nothing of the sort. It was important that she find out as much as she could from Shirley Smith. Could she also ask Sanjeve Patel if they have milk delivered? The brother Mickey Smith, Adams was unhappy they had not spoken to him yet, needed to know his whereabouts.

With both hands full, Gill had to push open the door to the relative's room with her foot.

"You've just missed Uncle Mickey. He was on the 'phone, the nurse wouldn't tell him anything so I had to speak to him. He's really upset at what's happened, said he would try and get back as soon as he could."

"Shirley we need to speak to him urgently as well."

"He's still abroad, will be ringing again to see how she is. I'll tell him you want a word." Adams would not be happy.

Shirley took her tea and sandwich. Sanjeve came out of the room, allowing Shirley time with her mum. Gill held up the other cup of tea, Sanjeve gratefully took it and sat down.

Gill asked Sanjeve about Jean. How did they meet? Sanjeve had a sister. Her and her husband owned a mini mart. His sister was unwell, needed help and Jean saw the postcard in the shop window. His sister knew how lonely he was. His wife had left him, took the kids and went back to her family in India can you believe it. Gill steered him back to Jean Smith.

"We just hit it off like. Shirley well she wasn't keen at first but came round, her mum was so happy see but that Wayne, waste of space. I don't bother speaking to him. Thick as you know what."

"What about Jean's father, did you get on with him?"

"He was worse than Wayne. Racist pervert. Interfered with all of his kids and other people's kids by all accounts, what sort of man could do that? Me I wanted to punch his lights out but Jean didn't want me involved, said he could be nasty. Anyway, she said Mickey would sort it."

"Have you met her brother?"

"Freddie yes. Took her to the prison a few months back to see him. He sent her a Visiting Order. She wasn't going to bother using it but I said she's stood up to her old man, now she needed to finish what she started and stand up to her brother."

"I actually meant the other brother Mickey Smith."

"No. He's out of the country most of the time. He always rings her. There's a number she can ring in a real emergency but it's not written down, very secretive he is but generous, anything she wants, he gets for her. Even helped out with the money for my taxi on condition I don't pry. All right by me."

"By the way. Do you have your milk delivered?"

"Where we live, you must be joking, be nicked before it reaches the step."

Chapter 25

Gill Cole was starving when she arrived back at the station. Sanjeve had been grateful for the sandwich, her sandwich. Why did she have to buy herself a cheese one? His religion, he wouldn't have wanted beef.

The incident room was buzzing. Gill recounted her conversations with Sanjeve Patel and Shirley Smith. Adams pointed out that the allegations against William Smith were still only hearsay. No one person had actually come forward and admitted being abused. Sheepishly, she told them about missing Mickey Smith on the telephone by a matter of minutes but he was aware they needed to speak with him urgently.

Jake raised his hand.

"It's not school. You've something to say, just say it."

"What I don't understand is how did he know?"

"Who?"

"The brother. If he's abroad, how did he know? It's only just happened."

****

Freddie was getting edgy. Things were happening and nobody would tell him what. He had been left with a couple of plods fresh out of training. Pinky and Perky well that's what he called them, laughed at his own joke. He only needed to hang on a little longer then he could be away on his toes. He had no intention of going back, would have no need to. Once he got his hands on the sealed envelope he would be in the money, move right away to somewhere warm.

The Driscolls, they were his priority at the moment. He needed to do something about them. They needed to know he wasn't a grass, at least not a grass where their business interests were concerned. They had long memories and their influence outside was even longer. He didn't want to be looking over his shoulder for the rest of his life.

While in Elmley, he had done his best to keep them sweet. Had been tipped the wink by an older lag. The cousins ran everything within all three prisons on the island, took a piece of all the action going on.

The Driscoll families had been travellers in the fifties and sixties, like his old man. They gave him their protection but in return he was expected to run the odd errand, particularly when he was transferred to Stanford Hill, the category D prison on the site.

There had been some trouble with their drug supply on the outside and they had wanted Freddie to meet up with their courier. Had even arranged for him to be assigned to the gardens where he could slip away unnoticed. He had agreed that he would do this one last thing before he got out. He would have paid his dues to them, go outside owing nothing. But their courier never made the meet. He was murdered. Freddie Smith told Danny Driscoll this while having his hand held over a hot plate in the kitchen.

He had done as they asked but the courier had been a 'no show'. Waited as long as he could before slipping back into the prison. He finally managed to convince them of his innocence in the matter, particularly as Sean had received news from the outside. The courier had been flashing his money about in the Admiral Nelson, Blue Town, annoyed a number of the locals.

All this business with his old man, the police coming to see him well it looked suspicious, made him look like a grass. He was becoming irritated, not knowing what was going on.

"So where's Batman and Robin then?"

"Detective Sergeant Adams shouldn't be much longer."

"How about a brew then?"

"Great, I take two sugars, my mate here has three." Freddie sighed; he walked right into that one.

On the way over Adams decided not to mention to Freddie that Jean was in hospital. No point, they didn't get on and he would be the last person she would want to see.

"But sir, what if he had something to do with it?"

"Not likely, has an alibi thanks to us."

They arrived at the safe house to find the front door open. Carefully Adams pushed the door fully open and quietly entered the hallway. Voices were coming from the kitchen. He thrust the door open causing it to bang against the wall. The startled officer spun around to face him.

"So tell me son what part of the phrase 'safe' house do you not understand?"

The young constable looked up puzzled.

"The front door, left wide open. Not particularly safe." Embarrassed, his colleague mumbled something about burnt toast and the fire alarm.

"Come on Freddie, no time to sit and chat, you've work to do today." Not even giving him chance to finish his brew, they were on the road.

Adams rang the Duty Sergeant. He wanted both constables off the team and asked him to explain to them the importance of honesty, particularly to a supervising officer. The desk sergeant said he would call back with the real reason the door had been left open. Angry, he had been humiliated by his boys in Adam's eyes.

They were soon on the M25 into Kent. Detective Inspector Dave Spencer had already been advised they would be on his patch. He had offered one of his cars but they declined. Adams had had enough of being looked after by Kent's finest. Dave Spencer advised them the new bridge over to the island was now operational. Be sure to use it, the view from the top was amazing.

"How do you know we are going to the island? It could be anywhere in Kent."

"Educated guess. Too much of a coincidence for it not to be."

Dave Spencer was right. The view from the top of the new bridge was amazing. Jake marvelled at the view of the wet grassland of Elmley Marshes. He remembered as a youngster his father Jacob bringing him down. Jacob had been a keen birdwatcher. He had tried to get his partner interested but Michael was a townie, give him an outside bistro table people watching every time.

Freddie directed the driver to the hamlet of Harty. In reality Harty was a small island with spectacular views over the Estuary towards Whistable and Faversham. At one time it had been quite a thriving rural area. There had even been a ferry to cross to the mainland from there. Now, only the Church of St Thomas the Apostle, a few derelict cottages and a public house remained.

"The body is buried there."

"You're joking, it's a bloody churchyard. Lots of bodies are buried. You'll have to do better than that. We're not that far from the prison, we can always drop you back there."

Freddie explained the old man told him that there had been a freshly dug grave. The body was flung in the hole and a covering of earth put over it. All they needed to do was check who had passed away and was buried in 1966, so simple even a copper could manage it.

Adams rang Dave Spencer. They would need an exhumation order and details of the deceased's living next of kin.

The relatives were not happy. Adams explained they would not be disturbing the coffin of their loved one, just needed to lift it. They were assured it would be replaced with care and as little disruption as possible.

Due to the high profile of the case it was decided to use the Forensic Science Service rather than their own facilities. The service had a state of the art mobile laboratory so the remains could be removed as quickly as possible. As the body had been there quite some time very little of the clothing remained. Thank goodness for the fashion for white plastic boots in the sixties.

Jurisdiction over the remains was argued above the heads of Adams and Dave Spencer. The fact that it may well be the remains of Monique Cecile meant that Adams had first call. Should the remains not be hers then Dave and the Kent

Police would take over any further investigation.

"Dave, sorry mate what can I say. Not our call."

"Yes you look gutted about the whole thing. This case could make whoever breaks it you jammy sod." Adams grinned.

"Can't say much at the moment but I may be able to help with your murder." They shook hands. Adams and Jake got back into their car and followed the mobile laboratory back over the new bridge.

Adams checked his messages. The Duty Sergeant had spoken to his lads. They admitted that Freddie had popped out for a few minutes. He left the door open so he wouldn't need to disturb them when he came back. They had been watching one of the porn films Freddie had requested. He didn't go far, was back inside five minutes.

"I'll leave you to complete the formalities with the Forensic people. I've already turned down lunch with Christine today, I'm not missing out on dinner."

Well at least Jake knew where he would be if needed.

"Oh yes, if James Macdonald turns up before they leave for heavens sake don't let him near the remains. The chaps from the Forensic Science Service don't look too kindly on other pathologists muscling in on one of their assignments. We don't want to upset them; they are costing almost the entire budget for this investigation."

"Great, that's all he needed, a turf war over the remains."

Chapter 26

The meal had been Indian. Adams didn't care very much for Indian, preferring Italian or just plain English, still no matter, it wasn't the main reason he was there.

The timing needed to be just right. He had eaten a decent meal, finished off the bottle of red and seemed sufficiently mellow. Trying to keep the anxiety from her voice she went for it.

"So how is the woman who took the overdose?" Adams looked up in surprise. He must have told her about Jean Smith over the 'phone, the reason he was unable to have lunch with her today.

"Holding her own at the moment. The next few days will be critical."

"Her poor family they must be worried sick."

"Her daughter and her partner are taking it in turns at the hospital. She has a sister but she is in a home, simple you know. I supposed someone will have to visit the home she's in, she'll have to be told as well." Christine hesitated for a moment unsure how to phrase the words.

"I saw her you know. Today I mean at the hospital."

"What were you doing there?"

"I have a contract with them remember. It's due for renewal soon. I went to see if there was any more work to be had. I was supposed to see a Ms Jones but she was too busy at some meeting or other."

"Did you see a policeman sitting outside?" Adams had given orders that there was to be a police presence at all times but knew what uniform could be like.

Christine nodded her head, not wanting to get the young constable in any trouble. Jean's daughter needed to pop home to collect some things and he had obliged. She had offered to wait outside the room, was waiting for someone anyway. It would be their little secret. He didn't see why not after all, she was a personal friend of Detective Sergeant Jonathan

Adams. He had been grateful, wouldn't be more that ten minutes at the most.

She looked so ill. Tubes sticking out of her body, attached to monitors and drips. Machines bleeping and flashing and the constant hum of the ventilator breathing for her. Gently stroking her head, Christine stared at her roots. The natural dark colour beginning to grow through. Same colour as me she thought. Jean looked old before her time, face heavily lined. Christine was glad she had given up smoking before it had done too much damage to her skin. It could so easily be her looking old before her time. She had waited so long for this moment, meeting her little sister, just wished it had been in different circumstances. As she leant over the bed Christine kissed her gently on the cheek and whispered in her ear.

"Jean hang on in there. Think about your boys. Boys need their Nana to look out for them. I need you, we all need you."

"Told you we wouldn't be long." Shirley stopped abruptly just inside the room, she had been talking aloud to her mother.

"What are you doing in here? Get away from my Mum, who the hell are you anyway?"

"Sorry, I offered to wait with her while the young policeman gave you a lift home, I was only trying to help. I would have stayed outside but I thought she had woken up."

Shirley looked at the well-spoken woman standing in front of her. She noted the expensive clothes. She seemed strangely familiar but she was far too worried about her mother to take in what she had seen.

Christine touched her arm as she walked out the room. Shirley held her gaze a moment longer than necessary, what was it? She couldn't recall.

*****

Sat down on the sofa next to Adams, she snuggled up

135

asked him about the rest of his day. That's what he liked about her. Doreen only ever went on about babies and settling down. Christine wanted to know about him, his day. He had her undivided attention.

He told her about finding the possible remains of Monique Cecile. He Jonathan Adams had the chance to solve a murder that had left others baffled. This could be the one to make him up to Inspector.

"But what about the other murder, the traveller chap. The one that Jake's working on with you?" Adams turned and smiled. She really had no idea of the ways of police work and why should she, a lady like her.

He explained that both cases could well be connected. He would be working on them together. Jake would be assisting him of course. He had begun to realise the depth of feelings Christine had for her stepson.

"Jonathan you are so clever. I'm sure I would be hopeless at such things." She walked into the kitchen to put on the coffee.

*****

Something was seriously wrong. Breakfast was late, the milk didn't arrive on time and when it did arrive, they forgot the eggs.

They always had eggs delivered on a Monday morning, then again on a Wednesday morning. New bloke, didn't really know the route, had been pushed in at the deep end. The usual one apparently hadn't turned up for work this morning, the dairy manager was not happy having spent most of the morning fending off irate customers. Mary began to have a panic attack.

Albie. Had he been taken in for questioning? Were the police coming to get her too? She was physically sick. Jean would know, what had happened. Jean always talked to her as if she were a normal person. She never answered her, just listened. Jean would come after lunch.

The Veg' Man called on Monday afternoons. Jean would always buy fruit from him for the boys and then she would follow him down the corridor to the day lounge. Jean knew about the importance of routines to her, often waiting patiently for the Veg' Man to arrive before she came to see her. But today she didn't come. Mary hated her routines upset.

If she couldn't make it, Shirley would pop in and tell her so. Shirley was always nervous around her, unsure what to say. The boys, well she loved it when they brought the boys. They took her at face value, never judged. But even Shirley never came.

What could she do, she was 'autistic', unable to communicate. It had kept her safe all these years, would keep her safe if they got too close over the old bastard's murder but she needed desperately to know what had happened to Albie and why Jean had not come.

The shift changeover was at eight o'clock. The night shift were lax, preferred to watch telly in the lounge rather than keep an eye on the residents. She would sneak into the office and call Albie. He had given her a number for use only in a crisis. He said the person at the other end would get word to him. He never carried a mobile himself, was convinced that it would be used to insert someone else's thoughts into his brain.

It was *Midsomer Murders* this evening. They all liked that, staff and residents, it would be safe to make the call then. They were supposed to lock the office but never did. She slipped quietly in locking the door behind her.

The number was picked up after only three rings. They did not announce who they were at the other end but waited for her to speak first.

She opened her mouth, nothing came out.

Chapter 27

Showered and changed out of his dark suit, he glanced at his watch. Six minutes to spare and he had taken the trouble to order proper flowers this time, not bedraggled pinks from the garage. It had caused him some ribbing when they were delivered to the station but they were beautiful, well worth the effort.

The meal was superb and Christine spent most of the evening flirting outrageously with him. As she leaned over to pour him a glass of wine, he had a vision of what was to come, perfectly formed breasts encased in a sexy bra that left little to the imagination.

At last for once, everything was going as he had planned it.

Christine had taken his hand, guiding him upstairs to her bedroom. He even got as far as sitting on the edge of the enormous bed, bouncing up and down testing how comfortable it would be. He calmed himself down, could feel the stirring in his loins. He watched as Christine opened a drawer and removed a skimpy silk chemise. She smiled at him as she wandered over to a door the other side of the room.

Adams slipped off his jacket, placed his mobile phone and keys on the bedside table and began to remove his tie. Thoughts began to race around in his head. What if he wasn't as good at it as her 'soul mate'? Nah, he was good, he knew he was. Even Doreen had told him on occasions his lovemaking was different, inventive.

Christine was in the en suite, slipping into the garment she had removed from her drawer. She had smiled at him said she needed to slip into something more comfortable. Sexy, he preferred sexy rather than comfortable.

He checked his wallet, the condom still in its use by date, just. What if he was expected to perform more than once, he only had the one condom with him. It didn't do to presume.

The first reaction was to ignore the noise sure he had turned it off already. He had it on vibrate and it want gently rocking on the bedside cabinet. Only when it lit up did he notice the caller identification. Even though he was off duty, he knew he had to answer it.

"Shit! It had better be good."

"Come on girl you can do this. It's not as if he's ugly, at least he's young and reasonably fit. You're just out of practice, that's all." Christine sprayed herself with 'Deep Red' by Hugo Boss. It had been a gift from Jake. She peered into the mirror. She still didn't look her age. Taking a deep breath she walked into the bedroom.

"Sorry to keep you waiting, but it will be worth it..."

Adams had fled, obviously not.

Jake knew he was under orders not to call Adams this evening unless his life depended on it. His life depended on it.

He hung around outside the building waiting for him. It was pure chance he had heard what was going on. Happened to be in a toilet cubicle when he took the call on his mobile. He didn't have the clout to interrupt the meeting going on inside but Adams did. It didn't take him long, must have gone over the speed limit to arrive so quickly.

"Bastard, old boys together. Well we'll see about that." Jake followed Adams into the building.

The two men were sitting in the office drinking coffee, sharing a joke. They looked up as Adams entered.

"Mother's meeting or can anyone join in?" James Macdonald coloured but was determined to stand his ground.

"Involving the Forensic Science Service is not a slight on your professional capability James but they have far superior facilities than we have."

"Bryan is a friend. I've asked him to look into it on my behalf. He is a higher ranking officer than you and is seconded to the Finance Division. I understand from Bryan that the cost for the FSS is way over the costs budgeted. I don't think it unreasonable as the Senior Pathologist to request the assignment."

Detective Inspector Bryan Low grinned at Jonathan Adams, this could be the chance he had been waiting for to get his revenge.

"Inspector Low has formally requested me to take over the autopsy and I have agreed. The Forensic Science Service will not be required now as I understand it. And to think, Adams gave up a night of passion with Christine for what, to massage a bruised ego." Bryan Low stood his ground and spoke to Adams.

"You haven't got your guardian angel looking out for you now."

"I think you'll find he has, now bugger off before I have you directing traffic."

"Evening sir, knew you wouldn't want to miss this one." Detective Chief Superintendent Arthur Fisher was not best pleased. It was bad enough being dragged out to referee a spat between two of his senior officers but to involve a pathologist of James Macdonald's seniority was unforgivable.

"James I'm really sorry you were dragged into this." He assured the pathologist both officers would be disciplined. James Macdonald thanked him for his consideration. Stupid old fool didn't even realise that Bryan Low was doing him a favour. James Macdonald had been very put out that he hadn't even been considered to carry out the autopsy. Felt that it reflected badly on his professional competence.

"If I can be of help to the F.S.S. myself and my laboratory are at their disposal." Adams told him it wouldn't be necessary. The remains were to be examined at the Society's state of the art research laboratory in Birmingham.

"I'd like to see the autopsy report when it's available, professional curiosity you understand." Adams said he would see what he could do.

Jake accompanied Adams and Fisher back to the car park.

"Freddie Smith, can we legitimately keep him after tomorrow?"

"Not sure quite honestly. He's a good brief in Andrew Giles. Unless he's helping us with enquiries then we can hold him a little longer."

"Have we anything we can hold him on them?" Adams thought for a moment.

"We don't but I could have a word with Dave Spencer. I'm sure they could hold him on suspicion of being involved in the death of George Parker."

"Any evidence?"

"None whatsoever but that didn't stop us in the past Guv." Arthur Fisher smiled, remembering the young Adams eager to make his mark, cutting the odd corner on his orders.

"Those days are long gone. By the book these days."

Inspector Dave Spencer of the Kent Police was reluctant to help. Adams had not been that forthcoming with the flow of information promised. Why should he put his job on the line for him? Adams had to admit, he did have a point.

Chapter 28

No point in hanging around the office waiting for the autopsy report. The boffins in Birmingham were the best; they wouldn't be rushing it. Monique Cecile's dental records were on their way, the final confirmation they needed to go public. Adams had personally arranged for them to be couriered up to them. He reflected on his spat with Bryan Low and James Macdonald. He had made two powerful enemies and at the moment he needed all the friends he could get. Arthur Fisher was due to retire at the end of the year, then he would have no senior officer fighting his corner.

Adams knew he shouldn't have got involved, left Arthur Fisher to sort it out. He felt bad about his unprofessional behaviour in front of Jake, not a good example, coupled with the fact he may tell Christine he had a short fuse. Mind you, he had never really taken to James Macdonald, found him condescending and patronizing. Adams hadn't gone to the right school and he didn't use the proper handshake.

Still what's done is done. With Jake, he headed over to the safe house.

"Time to have another go at Freddie."

"We've only got today sir."

"Jake you have this knack of stating the obvious." Jake mumbled his apologies. He had staked his loyalty to Jonathan Adams, even carried out duties that could be conceived as questionable for him. He just hoped he had made the right decision.

Freddie had only just showered when they arrived. One of the uniformed officers had gone down to Macdonald's to get their breakfast. They sat and waited for his return; Adams hiding his annoyance yet again that his instructions had been disregarded.

"Right you two lads, back to the station. Jake and I will keep Freddie company for breakfast,"

"But…"

"And you can be grateful that I'm not going to mention to your sergeant that you have disobeyed instructions. Two officers with the prisoner at all times I seem to remember."

"I'll not be in protective custody much longer."

"Eat your breakfast before it gets cold, we'll talk afterwards."

"While young Jake makes a brew, you and I Freddie, will retire to the drawing room, start our little chat." Jake groaned he didn't even like tea that much, well not the rough stuff Adams always wanted to drink.

"Your sister Jean, would she have known where the body was hidden, what with her and your old man being so close?"

"Why?" Adams took his time answering, wanted to see his reaction.

"I shouldn't be in too much of a rush to leave protective custody."

"I told you all I'm prepared to unless my brief is with me."

"Jean is in the Maritime, same place as your old man. Only difference she's still alive just." Freddie couldn't hide his surprise. He wasn't expecting that.

"What's it got to do with me?"

"I think it may be more to do with the murders of William Smith and Monique Cecile." Freddie was silent; he needed time to think. It hadn't occurred to him that his old man might have been topped because of what he knew.

"I need to go to the kazi'."

"You know where it is. Me and Jake will still be here when you come out."

The bathroom was too small to pace so he sat on the edge of the bath. The old man may well have told Jean about the churchyard. He wouldn't have told her about the powerful people involved though. He only told Freddie to show he was still the 'big I am'. Jean he didn't need to impress she was terrified of him anyway.

At his last meeting with Andrew Giles he had requested the sealed envelope. Andrew Giles had told him he had to

143

wait until after the funeral when the will had been read. He needed the sealed envelope. Needed to know what or whom he was up against.

Adams had threatened to have him put back into Stanford Hill. Perhaps it wasn't such a bad idea. Well yes it was. The death of George Parker had affected the Driscoll's influence within the prison complex. They needed to find out who topped Parker. If necessary they would beat him to a pulp to see what he knew. Danny Driscoll was a sadistic bastard, would do him serious damage just for the high it would give him.

Jean, he knew they didn't get on but she certainly didn't deserve what Adams told him had happened to her. Silly cow. He flushed the toilet.

"Tea's cold now Freddie."

"My brief's got something that belongs to me. He won't let me have it, says some rubbish about the will needing to be read first. Get me the envelope."

"Please. I need a lot more information before I go in with a warrant to a solicitor, professional suicide is that."

"I'll wait and take my chances."

"Like Jean took her chance."

Freddie made his decision. Blackmail wasn't his thing anyway, too much chance of being caught. He had to trust Adams, trust that he wasn't involved.

Freddie explained that his old man saw the killer a few years after he witnessed the body being disposed of. The bloke was giving evidence at the Old Bailey no less. Not a defendant a police witness. The blackmail information was to come to him when his old man died, that's why he was next of kin. In return, Freddie was to keep quiet about his perversions.

"This witness, was he a copper?"

"The old man wouldn't say, said he was someone important in the Old Bill. I would know when it was my time to take over the family business."

Adams set the wheels in motion to secure the sealed

envelope. Andrew Giles would be a formidable adversary but he was up to the task in hand.

*****

"Mary love, you've a visitor." She turned to smile but quickly averted her eyes. It wasn't Jean.

"Hello Mary, do you remember me, Julie Burton?" Mary shrugged and turned to face the wall.

"I'm afraid that Jean won't be able to come to see you for a while." Her body wanted to turn and face the policewoman, demand to know why but that would give the game away.

"Jean has had a sort of accident."

"What sort of accident?" asked the concerned carer.

"A suspicious overdose we think, not a self administered one. If she doesn't make it we are probably looking at murder." Julie had whispered the information but Mary heard every word. She clenched her fists and bit down hard on her lip wanted to shout out. Wanted to know how it had happened but in her heart she knew. Why didn't they just go?

"I'm not sure she's taken in what you've told her. Her Social Worker will be in later, perhaps she can get through." Julie gently touched her shoulder to let her know she was leaving. As soon as she was alone Mary stripped the bed and lifted the mattress.

She checked. They were all gone, only the little plastic bottles remained, he had taken the lot, made Jean swallow them somehow. How could he? He knew how much Jean meant to her. She would die for her sister, now it looks as though her sister might die for her. She needed to speak to Albie. Find out why he did it. Where had he gone?

Chapter 29

His personal secretary was a formidable woman adamant she would not let them pass. Warrant or not, the door would stay locked until Mr Giles returned. Even when Adams threatened to bash it in Miss Prim and Proper wouldn't budge.

The governor said to tread carefully so he had to wait in reception. After all she said he would only be ten minutes. Ten minutes for Andrew Giles to get up a head of steam and he knew just who it would be directed at. Him. How wrong he was.

A flustered Andrew Giles came rushing in, apologetic for keeping them waiting. He arranged tea for them all and escorted them into the inner sanctum as he called it.

Adams whistled appreciatively, he was in the wrong job. Either Andrew Giles was an exceptionally good solicitor or he was on the take. He knew what his betting money would be on.

"Yes it is nice isn't it? Most of the beautiful pieces in this room, I inherited from my father."

Adams gave him the warrant. He seemed to be expecting it, took some time reading through it. It was correct, whenever they dealt with solicitors and the like, he was always careful, checked everything twice and then once again.

"Inherit any clients from your father as well?"

"Well obviously."

"William Smith, one of these inherited clients?"

"You know full well, I really can't discuss clients with you."

"So he was then?" Andrew Giles, nodded, annoyed with himself for walking into such an obvious trap. He was sweating, nervous. Adams picked up on this immediately.

"All we really want is the sealed envelope that belongs to Freddie Smith. We don't really want to be poking about your files."

"The thing is, well we had a break in a few weeks ago. Just kids we think. Papers were scattered around, the petty cash was taken and a few files went missing, 'dead' files I might add. When my secretary told me what you wanted, I instructed her to get it out ready and you see, well it wasn't there."

"Three weeks ago today was it?"

"Well yes as a matter of fact."

"I assume you reported it?" Andrew Giles looked suitable embarrassed.

"To be honest no we didn't. There was very little damage and the files, well they should have been destroyed some time ago and it wasn't done."

"Same day as William Smith was murdered, what a coincidence."

"The Smith family, Freddie and Jean, how come you act for them?" Andrew Giles declined to answer until Adams pointed out the trouble he was in by not reporting a burglary of possible sensitive material. Wouldn't go down well with the Law Society.

"William Smith, well yes he was one of my father's clients. A friend in fact, they met through a love of boxing. My father was rather coerced into representing his son Frederick Smith."

"What about Jean."

"Jean is one of mine. Her brother who works abroad hired me. All bills go to him."

"Have you an address?"

"Not as such, I have a post box." Money is deposited in my account. I tell Ms Smith what the bill amounts to and it is deposited within three days."

"Paper trail?"

"No I'm afraid, it's always in cash. He works abroad a lot you know."

Adams thanked him for his cooperation. Outside Jake remonstrated with him for not pushing the solicitor harder.

"You heard the governor, tread carefully. Besides the

envelope is long gone." Adams asked Jake if he had noticed something odd about Andrew Giles.

"Not really."

"He was helpful, now that is very odd."

*****

"What do you mean it's gone? You've no right to keep it, it's mine I want it!" Adams quietly told Freddie that it had been stolen, but he didn't believe a word of it.

"One of your lot's involved in this."

"Are you telling me that it was the police who did the burglary at your solicitors?"

"Are you stupid or what? One of your lot did her."

Adams gestured to Jake to stop taking notes. It was a serious accusation and he didn't want any notes until he was sure there was some truth in it. He tried to explain to Jake his reasons, after he objected to being part of a cover-up.

"The problem is low ranking officers from the time of the murder would have climbed the slippery pole of promotion by now. It may be a senior officer. We need to get the facts sorted first."

Adams rang the office, spoke to girl wonder Paula Rogers, asked her to look up all officers involved in the original investigation who were still on the job. He may need to pick their brains, get a feel of what happened.

"Just police officers or support staff as well?"

This girl was good.

If he had been ten years younger nobody else would stand a chance. Oh, shit, Christine. In all the excitement he had forgotten to call her. He still hadn't resolved the problem of explaining his quick exit. Honesty had to be his best option, never used that one with a woman before. Dialling her number, he was diverted to the answering machine.

"Christine it's me. Look you must think me a prize idiot. Me, that's Jonathan Adams by the way," he slammed down the 'phone. Now she had proof he was a prize idiot.

Freddie had only told them what he needed to. Over the years he managed to get the full story from his old man. The bastard usually paralytic at the time, he never remembered what they had been talking about. He knew how it happened, where it happened but not the names. The names were in the sealed envelope.

Adams threw the mobile down on the coffee table, frustrated with the way his private and professional life was going at the moment.

Jake took the three mugs into the sitting room.

"Biscuits. We need biscuits. The mini mart is still open. Gingers will do."

"Sir, I thought you told the uniforms, two at all times."

"What about you Freddie? Gingers okay?"

"Long as they're not ginger beers." He looked at Jake.

"I'll not start till you get back. Be quick, your tea will still be warm."

Jake grabbed his jacket.

It happened so quick he caught Freddie off his guard. Adams grabbed him by the front of his jumper and pushed him back over the sofa, knocking the mugs off the table. He started to protest but Adams covered his mouth.

"Listen and you listen good. Either I get more co-operation from you or the Driscoll's are going to find out you grassed them up." Freddie struggled away from Adams and began to smash his face on the door-frame until he had the desired result, blood trickling from his nose. He grinned.

"I'll have you for this. Police brutality. You're a dead man."

"No Freddie, I think you'll find it's you who's the dead man. If the Driscolls don't get you, the killer of Monique Cecile will. He's already taken out your old man and attempted to take out your sister."

"Couldn't get gingers, got chocolate instead." Jake walked into the room and surveyed the damage.

"You are so out of the job when your superior sees what you've done to my face." Freddie turned hadn't noticed Jake come in. Jake took in the scene in front of him looking first at Freddie and then at Adams for an explanation.

"You better make up your mind son." Adams stood waiting for a reply.

"Never realised you were so clumsy Freddie."

Chapter 30

"I'm not sure if you can see her Sister. It's very irregular." Sister Bernadette would not be deterred. She had made a promise and she would keep it.

"I work in the community with God's damaged children. She will see me my child." The tone of her voice told the woman she would not leave until she had spoken to Mary.

Mary only had authorised visitors. She could be unpredictable, prone to violent outbursts, all this she explained to the nun but Sister Bernadette was resolute, she must speak with her. Mindful of her Catholic upbringing the carer opened the door wide and Sister Bernadette stepped inside.

"Thank you dear, which room is it?" She was shown down the corridor to a small room at the back of the house. A lovely room, it looked out onto the garden. Mary loved to look at the garden. Sister Bernadette tapped gently and then walked straight into the room.

Mary was sitting in semi darkness staring out a squirrel. She did not turn around.

Sister Bernadette spoke to her softly. She was a friend of Albie she told Mary. She had made a promise to him she would come and see her, explain why he left. His last intelligible words had been ask Mary.

It had not taken her long to track Mary down. Albie knew few people. Albie was unwell, a very tortured soul. He had been admitted to hospital in a catatonic state. His mind was in a place that only Jesus could reach.

"Albie, he was doing so well, then it all went wrong. He had taken Jesus into his heart, forgiven those who had done unspeakable harm to him but then he was lost again."

What had she done? No he said he wanted to do it, would never forgive them for what they forced him to do. She had nothing to feel guilty for.

Albie, he had betrayed her, looking for salvation from

his sins. Well she wasn't going to go down now. Mary snatched up the photo of her, Jean and the boys on the seafront at Leysdown. She stabbed at the photo and became agitated.

"What is it my child?" She screeched and wailed. The nun's pacifying hand was knocked away. She wanted to see her beloved sister Jean. She pushed her bed hard against the wall, making as much noise as she could. The duty carer came rushing in.

"I told you she could be unpredictable Sister, you'd better go now before I get into trouble." Mary had another go, jabbed her finger on Jean's outline.

"I think maybe she is concerned over the people in the photograph." Sister Bernadette you are a genius. Mary immediately calmed down and smiled at her.

"Well she's not done that before, made eye contact like that." Sister Bernadette understood, had managed to break down Albie Tate's defences, with time and the love of Jesus. She would visit Mary again.

"Her sister didn't visit yesterday, she looks forward to her sister visiting."

"Did anyone contact her sister to find out why she couldn't come?"

*****

She parked around the corner, the same as last time. She hated this part of the job, giving bad news. By rights it should be Gill Cole's call but Mary had met her, it would be better coming from her. She stepped to the side and smiled at the nun. She didn't acknowledge her, head down she was mumbling to herself. Probably saying her prayers thought Julie.

"She is a popular lady today."

"Excuse me?"

"Our Mary, you're the second visitor this morning. You must have passed Sister Bernadette." Julie ran down the path back toward her car. The tree-lined road was deserted. She must have had a car parked nearby.

"Think girl." Julie shut her eyes. She couldn't remember any other cars parked along the road.

"Call yourself a detective."

Before going into see Mary, Julie interrogated the duty carer.

"Are you sure she was a nun? Did you ask for identification?"

"Well no. It's not as if they carry warrant cards like you lot. Anyway, if you were unlucky enough to be taught by nuns, you can tell them a mile away, gives you time to get rid of the evidence. She was definitely a nun."

No she told Julie, she could not remember her visiting Mary. She did check the visitors' log – no Sister Bernadette. Julie asked why she hadn't signed her in today. Sheepishly, she admitted she was watching her programme, never missed it so didn't bother with the log. She was a nun after all. Julie wondered how many other visitors had not been signed in.

"She got a bit agitated earlier. Sister Bernadette seemed to think it might be something to do with her sister not visiting yesterday. Be careful she may go off on one."

"Hello Mary, do you remember me?" Mary continued to stare out of the window, refusing to acknowledge her presence in the room.

"I've come to tell you about Jean, why she couldn't visit yesterday." Mary turned towards her at the mention of Jean. Careful not to make eye contact though, she needed to keep herself safe. Julie could see tears running down her cheeks. She was mortified, supposed to have come over yesterday evening but they were late finishing so hadn't bothered.

"Jean is in hospital." Mary looked up fear in her eyes.

"Would you like me to take you to see her?" She nodded gratefully.

"I'll just let them know you're coming with me."

"You can't just up and take her out."

"This is not a prison. I am a police officer and she wants

to go see her sister."

"That one never knows what she wants. I'll have to speak to the Boss."

"Speak to whoever you like. If you want us we'll be at the Memorial Hospital." Julie went to collect Mary she was waiting in her room in her coat and outdoor shoes.

"So I did get through to you." Mary took hold of Julie's shoulder bag strap and followed her out. She kept her head down and stared at the pavement as she walked, careful not to step on any cracks, or bugs, or leaves. She hadn't been outside the home for quite a while; it was a little scary. But she was never scared when Jean took her out. Jean always made her feel safe and secure.

Julie took her time, allowing Mary to put on her own seat belt. She kept a tight hold of the belt as if her life depended on it. Julie radioed ahead; they were to go directly into the ward through the fire escape, less stress for Mary that way.

It didn't take long for them to reach the hospital. As they drove around the outside of the building, Mary glanced up at the fire escape for Nelson Ward remembering what they had done to the bastard.

Mary gave an audible gasp as they entered Jean's room. Julie thought she looked much better than before, at least she was off the ventilator now. Shirley stood to allow her aunt to sit down.

"I'm gasping for a fag. You staying with Mary?" Julie nodded.

Mary laid her head next to Jean, almost touching. Jean her special Jean, her heart was breaking. If anything happened to her what would she do? Jean loved her unconditionally as she loved her.

"Mary, I'm just going to get a cup of tea. Would you like one?" Mary didn't move.

"Don't worry, I'm just outside." At the sound of the door shutting, Mary grabbed the clipboard at the bottom of the bed. She recognized the names of the drugs she had taken.

Jean hated drugs, tried to persuade the home to cut hers down to the bare minimum. She had wanted to please Jean, had hidden the drugs they gave her. She never told a soul except Albie. He knew where she hid them.

Chapter 31

Jake took Freddie to the bathroom, helped him clean up but he angrily pushed him away. When they went back into the sitting room, the coffee table was upright and three fresh mugs of tea were waiting.

"You really haven't a full grasp of the situation Freddie. Let me explain it in a way even you will understand. You're damned if you do and you're dammed if you don't; and there's still the little matter of the murder of George Parker."

"Nothing to do with me, I was inside remember."

"What if I could put you at the scene?"

"I'd say you were fitting me up."

"This murder, bad for business or so I've been given to understand. Sean Driscoll's anxious it's sorted out as quickly as possible." Jake was beginning to think he had chosen the wrong side.

"Always knew you were bent." Freddie spat out the words.

"All bloody coppers are bent one way or another. Need to get my head right." Adams nodded, slow on the uptake Freddie would get there eventually. The doorbell rang.

"Meals on wheels have arrived. We'll be at the pub." The two uniformed officers nodded to them as they walked out the door.

Jake queued at the bar whilst Adams found a quiet corner. He had wanted to be a detective for so long and now it was all unravelling. Adams bent. He just couldn't believe it.

"You're quiet. Come on out with it." Jake composed himself, unsure what he wanted to say.

"Can't beat a good pint."

"Sir I think I may not be cut out for CID, I should like to return to uniform. I'll carry on with the investigation obviously."

"Will you now. What makes you so high and mighty that

you think you can dictate to the SIO?" Suddenly a light bulb flashed in Adams' brain.

"So. On the say so of the likes of Freddie Smith you think I'm bent. On the payroll of the likes of the Driscolls." Jake had the grace to go red with embarrassment, started to stutter.

"The evidence."

"Is circumstantial. Working with me these last few weeks, getting to know me, do you think I'm bent? Yes or no." Jake looked at him directly, Adams held his gaze never wavering.

"No."

"Good, can't have both of us bent now can we." Adams laughed at his own joke.

"How long have you known?"

"I'm a detective, how long do you think you idiot. Your sexuality is of no interest to me. What bothers me is that you are a good honest copper but mind I don't want you coming into work in make up or spandex."

The jukebox began belting out the Village People's YMCA. They grinned at each other.

"Freddie boy knows more about the murder of George Parker than he's letting on. I just want to put the frighteners on him. My priorities are his old man and Monique Cecile. Let's get those two sorted out and then we can worry about Dave Spencer's case.

"What about the attempted murder of Jean Smith?"

"It's not obvious, but I'll bet you that's connected too."

"Perhaps she knows, what Freddie knows."

"Perhaps but at the moment, he's all we've got to work with." With lunch over, they strolled back to the mansion block.

"So have you spoken to Christine recently?"

"Yes." Jake smiled to himself; he wasn't going to make it easy for Adams.

"Did she mention me at all?"

"Yes she did." Adams grabbed his arm as he pressed the

bell for entry to the main door.

"Easier getting information out of Freddie. What did she say?"

"Well she wondered if perhaps you were batting for the other side too. Apparently you fled as she was, what were the words she used, just as she had made herself beautiful and available."

"It's not like that and let me tell you something, I've had more women."

"Than I've had hot dinners, yes I know you told me before. Was that when you realised I was gay and thought I might hit on you?" Jake laughed. Adams smiled realising he had well and truly walked into the trap.

"Relax sir, I told her I had called you away on a matter of life or death."

"So if I call her, she would speak to me?" Jonathan Adams uncertain of himself, this was a side Jake hadn't seen before, very scary.

This time, the door to the flat was shut and they had to put their warrant cards through the letterbox before it was opened. They must have had a right 'bollocking' from the Duty Sergeant. They waited until the two uniforms had left. Adams handed over the bottle of Stella and packet of Bensons and Hedges he had purchased on the way back.

Freddie was now more relaxed. He had decided what course of action he would take. He knew the beer and cigarettes were a way of buttering him up. He wasn't daft. The murder of his old man and the attempted murder of his sister had shaken him up more than he cared to admit. He decided to tell them everything he knew about Monique Cecile.

***

Shirley gratefully accepted the tea from Julie. They stood chatting, both glancing nervously through the observation window. Mary was still sitting with her head on

Jean's pillow.

"I'm not going to be responsible for her if anything happens to me mum. I told her that from the beginning. Uncle Mickey, well he's never around, alright him sending money but money ain't everything." Tears began to roll down her face. Julie put a comforting arm around her shoulders.

"Don't upset yourself. I spoke to the doctor earlier. She's holding her own."

"I know, it's just that it's not my mum in that bed, just some old sad woman. My mum is brash, alive with life in her. She wears clothes too young for her. I'm always telling her to act her age but I would give anything just to see her with a mug of tea in one hand and a fag in the other moaning about the neighbours. I want my mum back." She began to sniff loudly. Julie handed her a packet of tissues.

"Standard police issue."

"Shirley, can I ask about the drugs. Where would you mother have got them from?"

"God knows. I can tell you she wouldn't have had that many hanging around in her house. My boys stay overnight. She wouldn't keep anything there that might be dangerous for them."

"Could they have belonged to Sanjeve?"

"Wouldn't have thought so, against his culture to use drugs, besides he's so laid back, he wouldn't have a need for them. If you ask me the low life who did this to me mum brought them in with him."

"Why do you think it is a man?"

"Me mum may be slight but she's wiry. Put down women much bigger than her when she'd had a few. No only a bloke could have done this." Julie thanked her, said she would come back later to take Mary back.

"Suppose I'd better go in and sit with Mary."

"Before you go can I ask you. Do you know a Sister Bernadette?"

"Mum might, I stopped going to Church when I met Wayne, too many sins to confess after that."

Chapter 32

"What you got to remember see, I got most of this information from the old man when he was in drink. Sometimes he boasted to make himself look big. It might not be gospel."

"I'm not a vicar, I'm not interested in gospel." Freddie drained the beer can. Held it up enquiringly. Jake shook his head, well it was worth a try.

"The old man saw it all go down. A cocky young bloke he said it was. Drunk, he kept pestering her. Looked like she had gone down to the car deck to hide but he must have followed. Had her up against the wall. Hand over her mouth, he lifted her dress and raped her."

"Didn't your father try to stop what was happening?" Freddie looked at Jake, was he simple or something.

"Course he didn't, got off on watching them stupid. He didn't have it all his own way though. Afterwards when he relaxed his grip she kicked him where it really hurt and gouged his face. Then the old man said he really went off on one. Smacked her really hard, even he heard it. She fell and hit her head."

"How did she end up on the Isle of Sheppey?"

"Bundled her into the boot of a car. The old man followed saw where he dumped her."

"Did he recognize the man?"

"Course not, never seen him before but he saw him again years later. He just couldn't believe it. Recognized him straight away. It was at the Old Bailey of all places. Can you believe it, the old man was there as a character witness. The bloke was giving evidence, working for the police. The old man thought that was hilarious."

"Freddie this is a very serious accusation, have you any evidence?"

"What do you think? Believe me or not, I don't give a toss."

Jake glanced down at the text message on his mobile.

"Sir, we need to put the local news on."

They just caught the tail end of the broadcast. Detective Chief Superintendent Arthur Fisher in full uniform filled the screen.

"We can confirm that a body found in Kent has now been identified as that of Mademoiselle Monique Cecile, her family have been advised." Fisher always went for the dramatic, his hobby you see, amateur dramatics. Made a great laughing policeman. He went on to confirm that an arrest was imminent.

"A little premature there sir."

"Premature! Not even bloody conceived yet."

"No pressure from the governor then sir?"

Although Freddie had given them vital information, the deal was nothing on the record for the moment. Adams had agreed. Freddie would go on the record when the killer was caught, safer for him that way and he would be able to claim the substantial reward for information put up by her family and a tabloid newspaper.

The clock was ticking, they only had until this evening then Freddie was free to go. They needed to be back in the incident room, pull all the information together. The uniformed officers returned.

"We'll get back to you later today. I may need to go over a few things."

"I'm not going anywhere, at least not until tomorrow."

*****

At Adams' request, all the team were waiting in the incident room, together with Paula Rogers the computer whiz. Adams started the proceedings. He outlined the need for discretion. There were to be no leaks on his team. Anyone caught passing information to an outside source would face immediate suspension and possible criminal proceedings themselves.

161

He mentioned the possibility of someone on the job being involved, the whispered chat stopped. Now he had their full attention. He gestured for Paula to come to the front and give her report.

Confident and unfazed, she began speaking. She had been asked to see which serving officers at the time of Monique Cecile's disappearance were still on the job. A titter went around the room at her choice of words.

"Settle down you lot, there are young impressionable minds present." Murmurs of 'sorry guv' went around the room.

"I also looked at other personnel still serving. They include a number of administrative staff, cleaners, maintenance people." A voice from the back interrupted.

"Guv, are you saying one of our own is the killer?"

"No of course not. The killer may be working within the police authority now but we will need to interview serving officers at that time, check nothing has been missed." A groan went out. Coppers were useless interviewees, questioned everything you asked, always on the defensive.

Julie raised her arm.

"Should have gone before assembly love."

"Very droll. Speak to me when you become a grown up." Adams beckoned her out to the front.

She had the report from the hospital. Jean had taken or been forced to take a number of drugs, not the sort, according to her daughter that would be kept in the house. Julie had talked at great length to the doctor; some of the drugs were of a type used to control mental illness.

"Autism?" queried Jake.

"Yes some of the drugs were used for autistic patients, particularly those prone to violent outbursts." She could see what he was getting at. She told them of Mary's surprise visitor, Sister Bernadette, she was still trying to chase her up for interview. Sister Bernadette cared for 'damaged children' but the carer seemed to think she had not visited before. Asked if any of the team had come across a Sister Bernadette during the course of other work on the streets. Silence.

Julie had left Mary at the hospital. When she mentioned taking her back to the home she had become very agitated, would not leave her sister. Shirley said she would stay with her. The nurses were happy for her to stay a little longer. Julie would be going back to collect her later.

"Guv, have we got the forensics back yet?"

"I'm still waiting the official confirmation but the remains have been confirmed as Monique Cecile, the French police have informed the mother. Apart from that I know no more than the rest of you."

Adams assigned the tasks and reminded them that Freddie Smith would be free to go after today so they needed to make progress like yesterday.

Those requested to stay behind watched as Adams wrote on a whiteboard, 'Killer 1? Killer 2?' They looked at him puzzled.

"It's just an idea. Anybody else got any thoughts on it?" They all shook their heads.

"The way I see it, with Monique Cecile, the killer just wanted to have some fun but she fought back, a spur of the moment killing. Macdonald has looked at the autopsy photographs for me. He is of the opinion that the fracture of her skull could have been caused by a fall. Most we could hope for would be manslaughter."

"And rape Guv, don't forget the rape."

"The rape is only hearsay, there's no evidence to prove it."

"William Smith is the connection. He could have been blackmailing the killer and paid with his own life."

"I don't buy that sir. Why kill him now? The killer has been paying him for all this time, unless William Smith wanted an even bigger pay packet each month there's no reason for him to take the risk." Julie quickly interrupted the conversation.

"What if William Smith was killed not for what he knew but for what he did to his kids and probably other kids too?"

"Jean Smith, she was abused not an abuser. How come she was almost killed?" Jake had a point.

"I never said it was perfect just a thought."

"Mary knows something but it's locked inside her mind. We need to find the key somehow."

"Gill I want you to concentrate on this Sister Bernadette, if she works with damaged children as she claimed then one of your sources must know who she is."

"Assuming she is a nun Guv.'

Jimmy Benton. Adams had a job right up his street totally boring but attention to detail was essential. Paula managed to pull together a list of passengers using the ferry on the day of the murder.

"I'm assuming she was killed on the ferry, if Freddie is to be believed. Can you cross reference it to people working with us at the moment?"

Jimmy took the sheaf of papers. It would take some time but he had plenty of that.

Chapter 33

"Got time for a quick coffee before you head back to the hospital?" Julie hadn't really but Gill wasn't the sort of person to just chat, she had something on her mind.

The problem Gill had was Sister Bernadette. Gill herself had dealt with problem families for ten years liasing with many agencies including the Catholic Societies. Never come across a Sister Bernadette working with problem kids. She asked Julie if the carer could have been mistaken, perhaps she wasn't really a nun. Julie checked her notes.

"The carer seemed to think she was genuine, reckoned she could tell a nun a mile away, they have an air about them apparently. My turn to ask you something, what do you think of the guv's idea of two killers?"

"I'm keeping an open mind for the time being. Are you coming back in after the hospital?"

"Is the guv?

"Don't think so, but Jimmy will be here." Julie coloured.

"You could do worse, he's fit and financially solvent, what more could you want?"

"A six pack and cute backside."

Julie took a small detour at the hospital. She was in luck the catering supervisor was still in his office. Something had been niggling her she told him and he could probably help.

"It concerned the morning of the murder. Ms Jones' swipe card was used a few moments before yours. On your statement you said it was definitely not Ms Jones but you couldn't recall that it wasn't a member of staff. Sorry, I'm not making myself very clear what I want to know is could the person in front of you be someone you recall from around the hospital?"

"Suppose so. I remember not being surprised by him using the door, so I must have recognized him as someone I see quite often."

"You said him. It was definitely a man." The supervisor thought for a moment.

"Yes it was. A young man, I've seen him about the hospital. Not one of my staff but I've seen him around. Shorter than me, I remember looking over his head toward the end of the corridor. His hair was brown and cropped really short. White, I remember he was white. I've a thing about coloureds see."

"Could he be a cleaner, porter, supplier, patient?"

"Sorry, it's gone. I had a hazy picture in my mind."

"Don't worry, it will come back when you least expect it. Here is my card, call me if you remember any more." Julie scribbled a few notes, young white male, brown cropped hair five foot six approx, frequent visitor to the hospital, shouldn't be too difficult to trace, just virtually impossible.

Sanjeve was waiting patiently outside Jean's room when Julie walked down the corridor.

"You come to take her back? She won't let me sit with my Jean."

"Sorry, I'm really sorry Mr Patel." Julie opened the door.

"Mary, you need to leave now. The doctors need to make Jean better they can't while you're still here. You can come back tomorrow, I promise." Mary leaned over and gently kissed her sister. Mary followed Julie out, head down, ignoring Sanjeve. The senior nurse had kindly unlocked the fire escape for them again. "She's going to be alright you know. It's very important that we catch the person responsible, they may try again." Mary looked at her surprised.

"Nobody has told you have they. Jean was given drugs, maybe even forced to take them. The person who did this is not a nice person. We need to catch them before they try to finish the job."

Mary began to rock to and fro and she let out an anguished wail. Julie began to fear for her safety while driving and stopped the car. Mary started to shake her head and a noise that sounded like 'no, no', came out. Julie turned towards her and took her face in her hands, forcing Mary to look at her directly.

"If you know anything." Mary dropped her gaze.

"You do know something don't you?" Mary nodded her head.

Back at the home Mary led Julie back into her room, lifted up the mattress. A hole had been made in the underside and Mary pulled out a plastic box. She handed it to Julie who found a number of empty bottles inside.

"Mary do you think that Jean was given your drugs?" She nodded and tears began to roll down her cheeks.

"Do you know who took them?" Again she nodded. Taped to the underside of her bedside cabinet she produced a passport sized photograph of a young man. She handed it over to Julie. Julie thanked her and promised she would do her best to make sure that Jean would be kept safe and she would collect her the same time tomorrow and take her back to see Jean.

On the way out, Julie showed the photograph to the staff; they all shook their heads but as one explained, they were the night shift. The residents rarely get visitors late evenings, it is discouraged, upsets the routine.

With all thoughts of going home gone, she headed back to the station.

Jonathan Adams had already gone home, well he told Jimmy that's where he was going. Jake had also left. His partner had done something special for him this evening and he was determined not to be late.

"Afraid you'll have to make do with me old girl." Julie smiled at Jimmy. Recently he had begun to allude to her as an 'old girl' as he put it. Gill said it was his way of justifying asking her out, kidding himself they were close in age.

"Is Gill still here do you know?" Jimmy looked at her with a hurt expression on his face.

"Women's problems Jimmy, don't want to upset your delicate stomach." That usually stopped them in their tracks.

"Think she's in the viewing room." Julie made her way down the corridor.

"Hi, didn't think you were coming back. I'm just about

to go myself." Gill looked at the grinning Julie.

"You've found something."

"Might have."

"Give!" Julie told her about the catering supervisor remembering a little more about the person who used the swipe card before he did. She also showed her the passport photo that Mary had given her.

"He has haunted eyes. Wouldn't be surprised if he wasn't abused as a young child."

"I'm not sure that Mary would have given it to me had I not mentioned that we are treating Jean as an attempted murder victim and the person concerned may try again."

"So the drugs belonged to Mary?"

"Yup, seems she has been hoarding them for some time. I checked the visitors' register. She had no male visitors apart from the doctor. Jean and Shirley are the only visitors listed."

"Get us a cup of coffee, I'll make a few calls and then we need to sit down and think this through."

*****

"Are you sure it's worth your while taking your coat off?" Adams stood shuffling at Christine's front door, with yet another bunch of flowers purchased from the twenty-four hour garage.

"Does the owner give you a discount on these now?" She laughed at his crestfallen face as she ushered him in.

"I thought we might start with the sex first, that way I'll just miss out on the meal." The look on Christine's face told him his attempt at a joke had been badly misjudged.

"The meal is ready, if you want sex as well, you'll need to eat quickly." A grin spread over Christine's face.

"Hope it's not too hot," he quipped.

"The sex or the meal? It's salad."

This time, Adams made it to the question, 'how was it for you' before the mobile began to vibrate on the bedside cabinet.

Chapter 34

Adams wandered into the incident room, smiling at all those he passed in the corridor. Nothing could dampen his mood today. Freshly made doughnuts from the twenty-four-hour supermarket, enough for the whole team and some left over for later.

Jake was already busy working at his terminal, cross checking names with Jimmy Benton. Julie had contacted him first unsure whether the information warranted bothering Adams on his night out.

"Right what have we got?"

Julie outlined her conversation with the catering supervisor giving them a brief description of the swipe card user. She felt sure she told them he would eventually remember more. She also detailed the information she had managed to elicit from Mary. She would go and see her again. Now that Mary trusted her she was hopeful she would be more forthcoming.

"So, this Sister Bernadette is more than likely to be the link between Mary and the person who tried to kill Jean. I'd bet money Sister Bernadette knows who he is." Julie closed her notebook and smiled at Adams.

"An extra doughnut for me I think."

Gill Cole stood up and began her report.

"I've 'phoned around a few old contacts from my earlier days. I think I may have found Sister Bernadette. In fact, I had dealings with her when I first came on the job but she wasn't a nun then just a streetwise little madam."

In those days Sister Bernadette was just plain Theresa Tate. Theresa was the oldest of eight children. The parents were drug addicts and the children ran wild. Their paternal grandmother was housekeeper to the local priest. The Tate children were fortunate the church took over their welfare. But she never forgot that early involvement in their miserable lives.

The passport photograph of the unknown young man was now larger; unfortunately, it had lost some of its definition but it was still an identifiable print. Jake positioned it on the whiteboard next to a photograph of Mary and Jean. Adams stood and moved the photo of William Smith and placed it on the same whiteboard. He connected them together with a red marker pen.

"We know from limited CCTV a slight figure we assume to be male was seen in the vicinity of the hospital at the time of William Smith's murder. Thanks to Julie we now also have confirmation that the swipe card was used by a man. My guess but don't quote me is that this is the man we're looking for." They nodded in agreement.

"Good work all of you. The pieces are coming together. I suggest you all get an early night. We're going to be busy tomorrow."

*****

Gill Cole had arranged to collect Julie from her home early keen to track down and interview Sister Bernadette.

"So has Jimmy Benton hit on you yet?" Julie glared at her companion.

"You could do worse you know."

"But I could do better. I'm thinking of asking Jake out for a drink." Gill smiled, best not burst her bubble just yet.

Sister Bernadette turned out to be quite elusive, not where Gill had expected her to be. Working with damaged youngsters most of her work was carried out at night around Piccadilly Circus, her office a small corner of Burger King. They eventually managed to track her down with the help of the Assistant Manager.

The presence of police at the hostel was making some of their guests nervous. They were asked to wait in their car whilst Sister Bernadette was woken and made aware they were waiting. She had been expecting them. Julie climbed into the back.

"So Sister, you live at the hostel?"

"The Lord lived among his flock."

"Yeah but not many of them were crack heads."

"All children are innocent in the eyes of the Lord."

As pre-arranged by Adams they took Sister Bernadette through the Incident Room, she glanced briefly at the blown up passport photograph. Julie waited with her in the interview room whilst Gill went to fetch a cup of tea and Adams.

"Can't be sure Guv but I think she might have recognized the passport mug shot."

Sister Bernadette was younger than Adams expected, dressed in a dark blue skirt, white blouse and navy cardigan. The only sign of her religion a large gold cross and chain and rosary beads attached to her belt. She noticed him staring at the crucifix.

"It's not real gold you know. I care nothing for material things. Besides, no reason putting temptation in their way."

Adams thanked her for coming in to help with their enquiries.

"That's what they say on the television and then you go and charge them with a crime. Do I need a solicitor?" The question threw Adams.

"Have you done anything illegal that would necessitate you being charged with an offence?" She shook her head.

"Sister can I ask why did you visit Mary Smith?"

"I work with damaged souls."

"How did you know Mary was a damaged soul, had you met her before?"

"A long time ago, in another life."

"Did you meet the rest of her family in your other life?"

"I recall very little of my other life. The Lord chose to take me away, my life is now with Him." Adams was becoming tired with the slow progress, nudging Gill Cole, the signal that she was to take over.

"How's your little brother Albie these days Theresa, still on the game?" Shocked Sister Bernadette looked up in prayer.

"Lord please forgive her, she knows not what she is saying." She pushed a copy of the photo across the table. Sister Bernadette glanced down.

"May I have some water and a little fresh air?" Adams terminated the interview. Julie took the nun out into the station exercise yard.

"Got a problem with nuns have you?"

"No Guv. She's running rings around us. She wasn't born a nun; she survived a hard upbringing. She's tough, needs to be dealing with crack heads and rent boys, just thought she needed a bit of shaking up."

"Quite right too."

Detective Chief Superintendent Arthur Fisher's personal assistant walked toward them.

"Sorry love, the coffee's run out."

"I'm looking for you. The boss wants you in his office right now."

"I'm in the middle of an interview."

"That's exactly why he wants you right now."

Arthur Fisher was not in a good mood. He had been well and truly 'bollocked', now it was Adams' turn.

"Arresting nuns are we now?"

"Sir?"

"Archbishop McDonald, has contacted the Chief Constable, who in turn contacted me. So are we arresting nuns or not?"

"Sister Bernadette is helping with enquiries sir." Adams explained the circumstances.

"Where's my report?"

"It all happened late yesterday. I've Jake Mortimer working on it as we speak. I think we're close to finding the person responsible for the murder of William Smith and the attempted murder of Jean Smith, just give me a little leeway sir."

"You've got as long as it takes me to receive my report."

"Thanks Governor." Adams hurried back to Gill Cole. He asked how long they waited for Sister Bernadette to get ready to go with them.

"Well Guv', she had to be woken; then needed to get dressed, about half an hour at most."

"Long enough to call people. Let's get on with it, time's running out." He stopped off in the incident room to get Jake to leave the report and help Jimmy. On the way back Duty Sergeant blocked his way.

"Orders from on high. The nun's brief is on his way over. No more interview until then." Adams looked at the Sergeant.

"Okay, I'm going for my break, I'll come and find you with this information in ten minutes."

"Thanks Dex I owe you one."

"No you don't, you owe me lots." Julie smiled at Sister Bernadette and stood in the corner to allow Adams and Gill Cole to continue the interview.

"Sister do you recognize this young man? I am of the opinion it may be one of your brothers."

"It may well be, I've not seen some of my brothers for some time."

"Well which ones have you seen?" Gill Cole had regained her composure she was prepared to be patient.

"Well Albert and Connor."

"Which one do you think the photo most resembles?"

"Albie" she whispered.

"A little louder please Sister."

"Albie, it looks like Albie." Adams nodded to Julie who left the room.

"Where is Albie now Sister?"

"Albie is ill, he's in a hospital."

"Which hospital, we would like to speak to him?" A sharp rap on the door quickly followed by the Duty Sergeant and Mr Andrew Giles, solicitor.

"You do keep popping up on my cases Mr Giles."

"Sister, pick up your belongings we are leaving. You have no right to interview my client without me present." But Sister Bernadette wanted to stay, knew her duty was to make them understand Albie, all his problems and his salvation in Jesus.

"Mr Giles, it wasn't a formal interview, no tapes rolling. Sister Bernadette offered to come and help clear up a few things."

Chapter 35

As an adult, Albie Tate had managed not to come to the attention of the police; at least nothing was held on him apart from a warning concerning his activities as a rent boy outside Piccadilly Circus tube station.

He came to the notice of Social Services as a feral child in need of guidance and protection but once he became involved with the Catholic Church nothing more was heard. The hard pressed Social Worker closed the file, grateful that the family was now someone else's problem.

Sister Bernadette told them how she found Albie again after all these years. He was a troubled soul but with the love of Jesus he began to live an almost normal life but something happened and he became lost to her and Jesus. His mental health deteriorated to the extent she had to commit him indefinitely. She visited Mary to find out what happened but was unable to reach her mind.

Andrew Giles presence in the interview room made it impossible so Adams thanked Sister Bernadette for her time and said they would keep in touch.

"I expect you to keep in touch with Sister Bernadette through me."

"Of course Mr Giles would I do it any other way?" The solicitor and his client both shook hands with him as they were leaving. Adams made a point of washing them after shaking Andrew Giles' hands afraid the dirt would stick.

"Guv, I've had a thought. Mary's home is run by the same Primary Care Trust as the hospital. If Tate worked for a supplier, he could be delivering to both places."

"Already ahead of you. Julie will speak to the day staff when she visits Mary. Gill I want you to visit the hospital, check with the catering supervisor, run Albie Tate's name by him. Whilst you're there check with the Psychiatric Department, you never know, just for once we might get lucky."

Julie parked her car and walked toward the Edwardian house. There was a different shift on duty. Two of them thought that the photo bore a resemblance to their milkman. They had no idea of his name; he never spoke to them, very shy apparently, just left the provisions and went. Julie rang Jake and gave him the details.

"Could Mary have had visitors without you knowing?"

"Possible, it's not a prison. We only log those who come through the front door."

"What about the milkman, would she have had any dealings with him?"

"Not very likely but he always parked around the back, would have passed by her window to get to the kitchens."

"She can be manipulative when she wants. Just because she's autistic doesn't mean she's stupid. Some autistic people are exceptionally intelligent, they just can't communicate." Julie turned to face the young woman who had just spoken. She asked her, what did she think that of Mary?

"She can communicate with you, you just have to ask the right questions in the right way. Don't assume she's stupid that's all I'm saying."

*****

Gill Cole had an interesting conversation with the Catering Supervisor. Yes he could well be one of the delivery drivers and yes he would be prepared to attend a line up if they found a suspect.

She saw the sign for Nelson Ward and on impulse decided to call in. Staff Nurse Joyce Lloyd was on duty. Gill showed her warrant card. The office was a little cramped but she was made welcome.

"Still here then?"

"Not for much longer, you know that bitch Tammy Jones had earmarked me to take the blame don't you? I'm a good nurse, it's all I know but when she's finished I'll be lucky to find work in a nursing home."

"We think that the murderer gained access to the hospital with a security pass that hadn't been reported as lost or stolen." Gill accepted a ginger biscuit with her tea.

"I'm still for the high jump."

"Not necessarily. The security card belonged to a Ms T Jones." Joyce Lloyd grinned at Gill.

"Did I mention to your boss when he interviewed me that there had been a complaint from another cleaner. From memory Mr Smith propositioned him. He complained to the owner of the agency he worked for but I understand they kept it quiet."

"Do you remember which of the agencies?"

"Same as the ones shifted on when he was killed. Thing is he turned out to be a student, a law student. Mind you, looked as though he should have still been in short trousers." This surprise Gill Cole, Adams had told the team the owner of the agency left everything to a manager, had nothing to do with the workers at the hospital.

The Mental Health Department was situated at the far end of the hospital. Gill Cole knew that they would not give out the information that she needed but she had a plan. She knocked on the sliding glass window to the reception office.

"Got flowers love for a Mr Tate, Albert I think."

The harassed receptionist looked up.

"We don't have a patient by that name."

"He could have been discharged. Would you check?"

"He is not a patient and even if he was, I can't give out that sort of information."

"Thanks. Didn't mean to put you on the spot. Thing is, this was my last delivery. Would you like them? Shame to let them go to waste. Can't be bothered driving back to the shop I'll just squiggle a signature, they never check." The receptionist was delighted with the flowers. She opened the sliding inspection window and looked about her before whispering to Gill.

"Technically, he was never a patient, left by private ambulance, almost as soon as he arrived."

She walked outside the building to make a telephone call and then walked back towards the Intensive Care Unit, picking up a coffee on the way.

Gill nodded to the uniform stationed outside Jean Smith's door and peered in.

Nurses were washing and turning her.

"No visitors today?"

"You just missed her bloke. He comes in at odd hours, he's a taxi driver."

As they left one of the nurses nodded to her to say she could now go in. Gill Cole quietly entered the room. Jean Smith's vital signs were monitored by an array of machine. She spoke gently to her.

"Jean, if you can understand me. We will find who was responsible for this. We think it was a young man by the name of Albie Tate," nothing registered. "He may be a friend of Mary." At the mention of Mary, one of the monitors began to bleep loudly.

"He may have wanted to be the only person in Mary's life." Jean began to thrash her arms. A couple of nurses came rushing in.

"You will have to leave. She's in distress." Gill mumbled apologies. An increase of the sedative dose was given and she became calm once again.

"You want to be thankful I'm not going to report you over this. She was in no fit state to be interviewed. I understand from Mr Patel it was you who found her and saved her life, that's the only reason you're off the hook."

"I assure you it won't happen again."

*****

Julie gently knocked on the door. Mary was seated looking out of the window. When she realised it was Julie, she stood ready to go back to the hospital.

"Mary, I need to ask you a few more questions. We will go to see Jean later this afternoon, just as I promised but I need your help."

Chapter 36

Albie Tate's personnel records from the dairy listed his address as a bed-sit. It was above the dry cleaners in the shopping precinct on the Abelard Estate, about ten minutes walk from Jean Smith's home. He could well have been watching the house for a number of days to know when she would be alone.

Armed with a warrant for his arrest, Jake and a number of other officers went to the precinct. When he received no answer to his knocking Jake went around the back of the building. He stood on the fire escape and peered through the grimy window. Albie Tate had not been home for a few days. Mail and free papers had begun to pile up. The manageress of the shop remembered seeing him about a week ago, reminded him the rent was overdue but hadn't seen him since. She assumed he was keeping out of her way until his money came through.

Andrew Giles had arranged a taxi to take Sister Bernadette home. He told her he had to see another client but in reality had requested a private meeting with Adams.

Off the record Andrew Giles told Adams about Albie Tate. He wasn't a client but at the request of Sister Bernadette he looked out for him. He wanted to explain about Sister Bernadette and her guilt about her brother.

Theresa Tate as she was then known had left her siblings to fend for themselves. She had taken comfort in her Catholic Religion to cope with their situation, her priest convinced she had the calling and she became a holy Sister. At the time the only other choice available to her was to go on the game. She saw first hand with her own mother what going on the game achieved.

It was only through her work with damaged children that she met up with Albie again. She was working with runaways and rent boys. Quite by chance she came into contact with Albie. At first he didn't recognize his sister but she did him.

Drugs had caused his mental health to deteriorate. Sister Bernadette did what she could to get him help; protecting him now was her way of making up for abandoning him when he needed her the most.

Adams wanted to know his whereabouts. If the information he required was not forthcoming Sister Bernadette would be arrested as an accessory to the attempted murder of Jean Smith. Adams left the solicitor in no doubt he would not take his client's word as gospel, if you will excuse the pun, just because she was a nun.

"But he's unfit to plead."

"He may be unfit but Sister Bernadette strikes me as lucid and in full charge of her faculties."

Andrew Giles opened his brief case and handed over a bulky brown envelope.

"The tape is a confession by Albie that Jean Smith had to go away, leave Mary alone. He was all Mary needed; he would take care of her forever. He was jealous that Mary loved her sister more than him. There is also a report by a Consultant Psychiatrist confirming that Albie Tate suffers from a number of mental disorders the main one being schizophrenia. There is also a private letter from Sister Bernadette for you.

All Sister Bernadette is guilty of is arranging a private hospital where Albie can be securely cared for. She had no idea what he had done, indeed didn't even know the existence of Mary Smith until he told her."

"How long have you had this information in your possession?" Andrew Giles shrugged his shoulders, told Adams the question was irrelevant, all the information he needed he had right there in his hand.

Andrew Giles stood to leave but Jonathan Adams wasn't finished with him

"We believe that Albie Tate may have also murdered William Smith."

"Not likely. Jean was a threat to having Mary all to himself. Premeditated murder; if you read his medical details you will see he is incapable of premeditated thought unless he heard voices in his head telling him to do it."

The police doctor was most helpful, gave Adams the number of a Consultant Psychiatrist, the best in his field. Adams emailed Albie Tate's details to him; he telephoned back almost immediately.

He confirmed the findings, he was unfit to plead. Adams asked him about autism. The psychiatrist told him yes it was possible for an autistic person to communicate if they had the will to do so. The idea that Mary Smith might have formulated and suggested the plan, planted the seed it was the voices in his head speaking to Albie Tate, was in his view plausible.

The only real problem as far as Adams could see was she never left the home unless it was for an outing with Jean. Mary Smith had never attended the Maritime Hospital, would have no way of knowing the layout of the hospital or that her father was there.

*****

Adams had arranged to take Christine out to a little Italian Bistro. He didn't trust himself at her home. She would want to make love and he wasn't sure he could manage it as often she said her Jacob did. She was already seated when he arrived.

He leaned over the table and kissed her on both cheeks.

"Very continental. I've not ordered but have chosen a nice white for a change." During the course of the meal it became obvious to Christine that his mind was on other things. She declined when the waiter suggested coffee. She had arranged a taxi; they could have coffee at her place.

Adams stood in the kitchen doorway watching her as she prepared the coffee.

She asked him how the case was going.

He told her it was now out of his hands. The killer was in a secure hospital in Ireland, all the paperwork had now been passed higher up the food chain. Just a few loose ends needed tidying up. Teamwork got them there in the end. Jean Smith would obviously be charged with being an accessory to the murder of her father when she was well enough to be interviewed.

Christine was impressed. She asked about the killer, what made him do it?

"I was hoping you could help me out on that one."

"Sorry, I don't understand."

"Well, one of my uniformed officers tells me that you visited Jean, spoke to her daughter Shirley."

"I told you I saw her."

"You never mentioned you sat by her bed holding her hand."

Adams said he wouldn't wait for coffee.

Christine stood in the middle of her kitchen as he walked out the front door.

*****

Jake had arrived home elated. They had the killer at least Adams seemed to think so. Such an anti climax, a written confession and Albie Tate's detention under the Mental Health Act. On The Bill it involved a car chase, a punch up and incarceration in the nick.

The vegetarian lasagne was defrosting in the fridge. Jake hated being the first home, looked forward to finding Michael there waiting for him. He put the kettle on for a quick coffee then heard the front door bang. Jake smiled, placed the meal in the oven.

"He let you off detention did he?" Jake smiled as he gave Michael a hug.

"We got the killer and he tried to murder Jean Smith."

"I'm all ears, do tell."

Jake gave him the abridged version, wanting to get Michael into bed as soon as possible. He explained that Jean, if she came round, would be charged as an accessory, may well implicate others too.

"What makes you think the sister is involved?"

"Sisters and brother."

"What?"

"Adams seems to think more than one sister and the brother is involved."

"On what evidence?"

"Michael you sound like a brief. It's done, file sent to the DPP. I don't want to talk about work any more. I've other things in mind. The lasagne will take another thirty minutes, time for a quickie."

*****

Mary retreated into herself. Julie was unable to get through to her. She talked to her about Albie Tate, how much he loved and wanted Mary all to himself. Told Mary that Jean was now safe. She had received news from her boss that Albie was being cared for. Sister Bernadette who came to visit, well she was Albie's real sister, looked out for him the way Jean looked out for her.

Sister Bernadette would do anything for her little brother, just as Jean would do anything for her little sister. Would Mary do anything for her big sister?

Chapter 37

Adams woke with an almighty hangover. After he left Christine, he had gone on to Jimmy's. In the early hours he called a cab, he remembered that much but very little else afterwards. Had not wanted a bad back and strained muscles to add to his general malaise. He didn't tell Jimmy about Christine. He felt stupid at being taken for a mug, didn't want his sympathy, told him the beers were for a celebration. Jimmy had accepted the beers but reminded him they still had the Monique Cecile investigation to finish.

He should have known it couldn't last. A classy woman like her showing an interest in him, there had to be a catch and boy it was one of the biggest. Bet she couldn't believe her luck when Jake was assigned to the case.

Jake, he was the real problem. How much of what had been going had he known about? Was he in on the deception from the very beginning? Jake had grown on him over the course of the last few weeks. Had shown real promise, reminded him of himself at that age. Not that he had ever harboured gay feelings. Perish the thought.

"Morning Guv." Adams winced at the sound of her voice, asked Julie to keep the noise down.

"Good session was it?" How that girl could remain cheerful at all times was a complete mystery to Adams.

The Consultant Psychiatrist had got back to him with regard to Mary Smith's condition. He advised it highly unlikely a jury would convict her as an accessory. It puzzled him how she was able to put it altogether. The answer was she hadn't. Others had to be involved.

"Morning sir." You see that's what he liked about Jake Mortimer, always respectful. Jake wandered over to Adams, lowered his voice.

"Christine was wondering if you were having problems with your mobile. She has left messages but you've not returned her calls."

"Battery needs recharging."

"Morning Guv. Good news, the hospital has just rung. Jean Smith's come round, we can talk to her." He smiled at Gill Cole.

"Anyone wants me, I'm in the canteen, stomach needs lining."

"Must have been some session he had last night." Julie looked at Jimmy.

"Nothing to do with me, he's a grown man."

Adams was sitting at a corner table, glaring at anybody attempting to engage him in conversation or share his space.

Arthur Fisher, his governor, wanted the final reports but at the moment he couldn't give them to him. He was still trying to figure out if he had compromised himself. Sleeping with someone involved would probably come into that category. He needed to find out why. He dialled her number, unsure what he wanted to say.

"So now you want to talk, well I'm not ready. You and Jake come over about six o'clock then we can talk." Before he could reply she had hung up.

Waiting for him on his desk was the official autopsy report on Monique Cecile. Cause of death was confirmed as a blow to the head. It could have been accidental but in the forensic consultant's opinion she was probably knocked to the ground. With a fall, you would put out your arms to slow the momentum, although both her arms were broken, he concluded that it had been caused by the coffin and earth directly above her.

He also noted there were a number of broken fingers. Either she fought back or she had been on the ground and her fingers were trodden on as a means of subduing her. These breaks were different to those of her arms. He also noted damage to the pelvic bones. This damage could have been done whilst the body was in the ground or could have been done whilst she was alive.

Just to add to his misery Freddie Smith was now out on parole. A room had been found for him at a halfway house on the Abelard Estate. He grew up in the area, felt safe there. The Driscoll cousins had very little influence on his patch. Solicitor Andrew Giles had made it quite clear to Adams that providing Freddie kept within his parole conditions he was a relatively free man and the courts would take a dim view of any harassment of him by the local police.

The Monique Cecile whiteboards had now taken centre stage in the incident room. The main picture was of a beautiful smiling seventeen year old. Long dark hair and deep brown eyes, she looked to have not a care in the world. Underneath were the pathology photographs.

Later today Adams was to accompany Mademoiselle Cecile to the spot where her daughter had been buried. The Kent Police were collecting her from Ashford International and he would meet them at Harty Church. He had already decided to leave early, had made arrangements to see Sean Driscoll in Elmley.

"Guv, the hospital's rang again. Jean Smith has discharged herself. Told the doctor her brother had arranged a private nurse. Said she would let them know where she would be staying."

"The bloody elusive brother I presume. Are you working on anything important?"

"Nothing that can't wait."

"Good you're coming with me this afternoon." Jake looked up disappointed that Gill Cole would be going with Adams. Gill looked across and shrugged, she had no idea why she was going instead of Jake either.

Julie walked across the room and touched his arm.

"He's not good with sympathy, perhaps he thinks he needs a woman's touch on this one, the mother." Of course, that must be it. Jake had seen Adams' attempts at empathy.

"You never mentioned we were visiting the prison Guv."

"Is it a problem?"

"Nope, it'll be nice to get some admiring glances for a change." Adams had to confess, he'd never looked at Gill Cole in that way.

Sean Driscoll was not surprised by the visit. He had been expecting Adams for quite some time.

"How's your old mum these days Sean?"

"Fine Mr Adams." Annie Driscoll had been mugged while Sean and his cousin had been banged up. Jimmy Benton had arranged for the culprit to be held on remand in the same prison. Adams had been a detective constable at the time. Jimmy was no longer in the job but the debt owed had been transferred to Adams.

"Did Freddie Smith ever mention a Monique Cecile?"

"The French girl found in the churchyard. You think he done her?"

"No but I think he knows who did."

Freddie Smith had disrespected Sean Driscoll. He wanted Freddie to know that it was he who had put him back inside. Adams agreed. He told Adams that a collection had been arranged on the day of George Parker's murder, so he had heard. Freddie Smith had run the errand, so he had heard. Passing on hearsay was not in Sean Driscoll's view being a grass. Just as he had suspected Freddie was in the area at the right time and unsupervised.

Adams looked at his watch. Told Gill if she put her foot down they would just make it in time to pay their respects.

"Guv, the Parker murder is not ours. Why are we interested?"

"We're not but I'll use it to put pressure on Freddie to find out what he knows about the Cecile case."

Gill Cole parked the car, and took the flowers she had purchased from the boot. Adams knew it was the right decision bringing a woman.

"Madame Cecile was in the back of an unmarked police car. Detective Inspector Dave Spencer helped her out. He had been peeved that the case had gone to the Met, the body had been found on his patch and by rights, the case should have been his. Nothing personal as Adams told him it's just that my boss can shout louder than yours. He nodded to Adams.

Gill Cole walked toward the elderly stooped woman and

spoke to her quietly, in French. She smiled, grateful for the small kindness. At the short ceremony Monique's mother said prayers, they stood heads bowed, respectful. Flowers were laid at the spot. Gill Cole came over and whispered.

"She wants to see the remains."

"Explain to her she can't, they're evidence. Tell her she can have her daughter back when we find the killer." She nodded and went over to talk to the distraught woman. After a few moments they came towards Adams and Dave Spencer talking by the side of one of the cars. She kissed them both on each cheek and Gill helped her back into the car. Dave Spencer accepted a lift back with Adams.

"So how's it going with the Parker investigation?"

"We're following up new leads and we've got a spot on next month's 'Crimewatch'. Understand you visited Sean Driscoll earlier, anything to tell me?"

"Wear a dark suit, makes you look more serious."

Chapter 38

Adams arrived back at the station with more than enough time to get to Christine's but was determined to make her sweat a little longer. He was still very angry at the way he had been treated. She had used him and involved him personally in an investigation. He could lose his job.

It had taken a while before it came to him. Christine described William Smith as a traveller. Adams never mentioned to her that he had been a traveller, the fact hadn't been reported in the media, so she needed to know more about him than she was letting on. The clincher was her omitting to tell him about the incident between William Smith and the student he propositioned.

He had been an idiot. Such a beautiful classy woman like that wouldn't be after the likes of him without an ulterior motive.

The door to the incident room slammed as he walked in.

Jake and Jimmy Benton looked up from the reports they were working on. He was about to speak to Adams when his mobile vibrating on the desk distracted him. Michael often sent him sexy messages but Jake couldn't remember the last time he had received ten in one day. He typed in 'me too' and then pressed 'send'.

Christine had telephoned Jake earlier, inviting him to dinner. Jonathan had been invited too. She asked Jake if he would mind giving Jonathan a lift as they were both coming from the office. Michael was entertaining a couple of his clients this evening so he was delighted to accept the offer of a meal even if Adams was the other guest.

Adams smiled at Gill Cole as she came in after parking the pool car.

"Good idea the flowers. Didn't know you could speak French."

"There's a lot you don't know about me Guv." She winked at him.

At six thirty Adams decided he could put it off no longer. He still had no idea what he was going to say to her or quite how he would handle the situation. Jake was waiting for him in the car park.

"If you don't mind me asking sir, have you and Christine had a falling out?"

"I do mind you asking." The rest of the journey Jake drove in silence.

Christine was waiting at the front door as they pulled up on the drive. Jake greeted her with a kiss. Adams just nodded a greeting and followed her into the living room. Waiting for them tucked up in a comfortable armchair with a blanket covering her legs was Jean Smith.

"I don't understand." Jake looked from Christine to Jean Smith and then Adams. Jean Smith looked directly at Adams.

"You want to know what happened." Jean struggled to get the words out. Christine handed her a glass of water and looked at him.

"You know don't you?"

"I know you are involved but not how deep." Christine took the glass from Jean and tucked the blanket tighter around her legs. Before she could begin, Jean started to speak

"This is my older sister. I've known she existed but never thought she would come looking for me." Tears streamed down Jean's face with the effort of speech and the sheer joy of finding her sister. Christine stood by the chair holding on to her sister's hand tightly, not wanting to let her go.

With a faltering voice she confirmed that Albie Tate had attacked her. She had no idea who he was at first. Mary, she remembered who he was, he told her. Helped him kill one of the bastards who ruined his life. Mary showed him the way to do it. His Mary not Jean's, she belonged to him. He forced Jean to swallow the drugs, said he wanted Mary all to himself. She passed out, remembered nothing else until she came round in hospital.

Adams looked at the shell Jean Smith had become; he

was sitting on the footstool directly in front of her. She grabbed his face so he had to look at her directly. Her eyes pleaded with him for understanding. Ignoring Christine, he told Jean about Sister Bernadette and the private letter she had left him, explaining why her brother was the way he was.

Albie Tate, had been brutalised by a paedophile gang of which William Smith was one. He had taken to drugs to blot out the pain and degradation. By the time Sister Bernadette found him his mental illness had taken hold completely. She took him under her wing and for a while he started to lead an almost normal life. He didn't mention that Sister Bernadette was Albie's biological sister Theresa, it was irrelevant to them and he had just about had enough of long lost sisters.

Meeting Mary had been the catalyst. Adams said Mary had put Albie Tate up to the murder but there were still some unanswered questions.

"We need to know about the plan." Jean smiled at him.

"I planned it. Our excuse of a father had to go. He arranged to move in with Shirley and the boys. She had no idea what he was really like. Jean told him how distraught she was about the new living arrangements. She had never told her daughter the sort of man her grandfather was. Ashamed her own daughter would think less of her." Christine placed her hand on Jean's arm interrupting.

"As soon as Mickey traced me and told me, I said I would sort it."

"I find it hard to believe that the elusive brother wasn't involved with the murder." No, Jean and Christine said in unison.

"I planned it when I found out who he was. I was able to gain access to the hospital through my cleaning contract."

"I wanted to do the bastard all my life, Christine had nothing to do with it. I planned it all on my own."

Adams was becoming confused.

"Albie Tate committed the murder, why are you both confessing now?" They were saved from answering by the doorbell.

Christine rose to open the front door, knew exactly who it would be. He walked into the room and stood the other side of Jean Smith. Jake stood open mouthed as his lover Michael smiled at him.

"May I introduce our brother Michael?" Michael walked toward Jake but he pushed him away. Tears began to run down his face; he hadn't expected Jake to reject him.

Christine implored Jake to give Michael a chance. She explained that when she met Michael and decided he would be ideal for Jake she had no idea that he was her brother. Michael confessed to her after he had fallen in love with the young policeman.

Jean Smith looked up at the brother who had taken care of her always. She had no idea that he was gay. The pain in his eyes was almost too much to bear.

Jake refused to talk to or look at Michael. Michael realised he had lost the one person who had made him whole. He turned towards Adams and began to speak.

"Jean and I talked about ways to change the situation. We would meet when she was out with Mary, we had no idea she could understand." Michael tears still streaming down his face tried to make eye contact with Jake.

"All I ever wanted in life was to look after my family, keep them safe from the bastard and his sick friends. I never expected to find someone for me. I had resigned myself to one-night stands for sex only. Then I met you Jake and found love, so overwhelming it took my breath away. I would die for you. I'll never love anyone the way I love you."

Adams coughed, now he was embarrassed.

"Jake, I need a lift." Jake walked out, acknowledging nobody in the room.

Christine grabbed Adams by his arm as he was leaving.

"What are you going to do?"

"Did you just sleep with me because I was in charge of the investigation?" She stood in the hallway with her arms by her sides. She said nothing; there had been enough lies already.

"Thought so." He slammed the door behind him.

Jake was staring straight ahead, his knuckles white on the steering wheel.

"First stop the off licence, then my place."

"What are we going to do sir?" Adams looked at Jake's tear stained face.

"Sort out this bloody mess."

Chapter 39

Adams wasn't sure what annoyed him the most. The fact that he hadn't twigged earlier or that he would have no more sex with Christine. Did she mean it when she said he was good? He thought he had been better than good, bloody amazing in fact.

He was seated opposite Jake in his kitchen. They never did have any food and Adams was starving. Jake just sat picking at his takeaway. He had said very little, still in shock, betrayed by the two people he loved and trusted with his life.

"What will happen when it all comes out?"

"It may not have to come out. Let's not rush into anything. We need to think about this very carefully." Unlike Jake, Adams had much to lose. Jake was young enough to start again. The job was all Adams had known and in truth all he had ever wanted. He'd be damned if a little indiscretion with Christine Mortimer would mean the end of his career.

He racked his brains trying to remember if he had disclosed sensitive information. He asked Jake if he had been indiscreet about the investigation. Jake shook his head.

"Not that I can think of. I loved him. How could he do this to me?" Jake began to cry. Adams was embarrassed. He felt awkward when faced with a crying woman; he was totally out of his depth with a grown man. He patted him on the shoulder in a manly way.

"Michael was looking out for his family long before he met you. He was already in deep before you became important to him." Jake looked up a grateful smile on his face.

"Wouldn't have had you down for a sensitive soul."

"Yes well don't tell too many people, I've a reputation as a bastard to maintain." Adams cleared away the remains of the meal, while Jake went in the other room.

In the sitting room Adams handed Jake a beer. Jake had already asked if he could stay the night. Adams had agreed provided nobody ever found out. He poured a whisky for himself.

"You need to ask yourself the question, what is more important in your life Michael or the job?" Jake took a swig of beer from the can. It had been the only thought in his head since they drove away.

"What about you, Christine or the job?"

"It's easier for me. We'd only had sex the once, good though it was, I'm not prepared to give up everything else for it."

Adams would prefer to keep his involvement with Christine Mortimer out of the investigation. He had been discreet, only Jake and Jimmy knew. Jake was already in deep enough without causing him problems and Jimmy, well Jimmy would back whatever decision he made.

Over the years Jonathan Adams has upset certain people. An indiscretion of this scale would almost certainly result in suspension. Detective Chief Superintendent Arthur Fisher was the only one fighting his corner and he would be retiring at the end of the year. As much as he wanted Christine Mortimer to pay for her deceit he knew he would do his utmost to keep her and Jake's boyfriend out of it.

Adams made strong black coffee; they needed clear heads.

"I'm not sure I can live without Michael."

"Well you can't have him and the job."

"Will he go to prison?"

Adams didn't answer him. He answered the door, went outside and paid for Jimmy Benton's cab.

"I see you've started without me." Adams had called Jimmy whilst waiting for the kettle to boil.

He looked at the two men.

"I can't believe you've cocked it up so badly."

"Tell us what we don't know Jimmy, we need a solution not a statement of the 'bleedin' obvious."

"We have a taped confession from Albie Tate, who is unfit to plead. We only have his word that Mary Smith put him up to it. Mary is also unfit to plead. Tate made deliveries to the hospital. He could have formulated the plan himself. Even Sister Bernadette said he had begun to live an almost normal life. We could argue that he made the decision to kill William Smith when he was rational."

"What about the attempted murder of Jean Smith?"

"That's easy. Tate also delivered to the home where Mary lived. He became obsessed with her, jealous of her sister. Just a coincidence she was the daughter of William Smith."

"Bit lame don't you think?" Jimmy looked at Jake.

"Listen son. Time like this you close ranks. I'm not about to let him take the blame just because you became involved with a devious family."

"Make your mind up time. What's it going to be, the job or your boyfriend?"

"It's not just Michael. Christine, she's been the only family I've had for quite a while." They talked around the problem until the early hours.

The world service blared from the bedside radio but Adams was already up and dressed. He took a black coffee into Jake, who lay naked on top of the bed. Adams stared, nope did nothing for him. He coughed loudly. Jake woke and pulled the sheet over his body.

Tired, his eyes puffy from crying, he had only managed a couple of hours' sleep. He took the steaming mug. Adams pulled back the curtains it was going to be a nice day.

"I need to know your decision. There are things to sort out." Jake rubbed sleep from his eyes.

"From as long as I can remember all I've ever wanted to do was to be a copper like my old man. Then I met Michael and he showed me there was more to life than just working. I can always find another job. I will never find another Michael." Adams nodded, it was the answer he had been expecting.

"Right then, you've ten minutes. Fresh towel and razor in the bathroom, we need to get going."

Whilst he was waiting Adams made a few calls.

*****

"Guv's late this morning." Julie made the remark to no one in particular. Jimmy looked up and smiled at her. She really was a buxom lass.

"He'll be in later chasing up a lead."

"Doughnuts." Gill Cole breezed in surprised to find only Julie and Jimmy Benton in the incident room.

"Was it something I said?" Julie picked up a doughnut.

"More for us. Grumpy will be in later. Don't know what's happened to Jake though." They both looked at Jimmy. Before he could answer them Arthur Fisher strode into the incident room.

"Jimmy my office now!" The girls looked at one another. They were used to Adams in a strop but Fisher. He was so angry, his eyes were bulging and he was shaking with rage. Not a word was said until they reached his office. Arthur Fisher locked the door and unplugged the telephone.

"Right bloody mess. I'm not sure we can get him out of this one." Jimmy nodded in agreement.

Chapter 40

Adams clicked his seat belt and turned to look at Jake. The shower had take taken the edge off his exhausted appearance.

"Are you ready for this? No change of heart?" Jake shook his head. Even with the soul searching deep down he always knew what his decision would be. He could cope with not being a copper but not a life without Michael.

They were not expected, that was obvious by the surprised look on Christine's face. Jake kissed his stepmother; she hugged him warmly. Adams just nodded in acknowledgement.

"Go through to the kitchen."

Jean and Michael were in the kitchen having breakfast. It was obvious to Jake that Michael was just as upset. Jake made eye contact with Michael, his eyes fearful of rejection.

"We need to talk." Michael followed him out into the conservatory.

Christine sat down; Jean squeezed her hand, she smiled gratefully for her support.

"Do I need a solicitor?" He looked at her for the first time. Why had he not noticed her hard steely determination? He told them what he had in mind.

Jake's relationship with Michael was to be kept out of the investigation. Apart from Adams, Jake's sexuality had not been disclosed and Adams wanted to keep it that way. Again, Christine's involvement with the Smith family would not figure in any reports, or his moment of madness with Christine.

Jean would need to make a statement regarding the abuse she received at the hands of her father. This would strengthen the case against Albie Tate. She would also be required to name others involved.

She looked anxiously at Christine.

"Don't worry. I'll get you a good solicitor. I've only just found you. I'll not let you go."

"Did your father abduct a small boy from a fun fair?" She nodded, tears began to stream down her face.

"He wasn't frightened, I was there you see. I was terrified. My dad said if they had the boy they wouldn't use me for nasty things. I didn't understand what was happening, all I knew was how terrified I was of him. The little boy, he came with us quite willingly. We took him to the main road. There was a big van waiting." She began to sob loudly.

"Can you tell his family I'm sorry? It was him or me and I was given no choice." Christine put her arms around her sobbing sister, telling her she would make it up to her if it took her the rest of her days.

"Somebody will come to see you, take a statement." Adams was determined to remain aloof from the family. At the sound of crying Michael came back in from the conservatory. Jake followed. He nodded to Adams and mouthed the words 'all done'.

"You really are a bastard."

"Maybe but this bastard will stop you and your boyfriend from serving time."

"Jake has nothing to do with this." Adams looked at him contemptuously.

"For an intelligent man, you really are stupid."

*****

Arthur Fisher had calmed down. Jimmy said he would talk to him until he was in a frame of mind to actually listen.

"Just think it through. We keep Adams and Jake out of the proverbial and we get to take out an extensive paedophile network."

"What about the Cecile case, we compromise that and even I'll be up to my neck in it." Seven months that's all he had left. Seven months of cruising and Adams had to pull a stunt like this.

"Didn't have him down for being led by his nether regions."

Jimmy Benton patiently explained the plan to Arthur Fisher again. The Monique Cecile case was separate to the William Smith murder; it would not be compromised.

"Get the reports on my desk. I'll push them upstairs then it's out of our hands."

"Thanks Arthur."

"Keep Adams out of my sight for the next seven months." Jimmy waived as he walked out the door.

*****

"Excuse me, I need to take this call." Adams walked out into the garden. It was the news he had been waiting for. He beckoned for Jake to join him.

"Michael thinks I should move to France with him. He's just bought a derelict chateau. It was to be a surprise for our anniversary. Christine has agreed to look out for the family. Christine, Jean, Shirley and the boys may even join us later."

Right now Adams was less interested in Jake's domestic arrangements and more interested in how they needed to handle things from now on.

He explained to Jake what had been worked out between Jimmy Benton and the governor. Jake was not to return to the investigation. He had a family emergency that necessitated he take a few weeks leave that was owing to him. He was not to contact any of the team.

A few weeks in France would be ideal.

"So I'm to be the one who takes the flack."

"You made your choice."

Michael joined them in the garden anxious Adams would try to persuade Jake to stay in the force. He was keen for Adams to be gone.

"Your taxi has been ordered. He was a nasty piece of work you know, my old man. Someone would have got to him eventually, he knew too much you see."

Jake went inside to see Christine. He hated goodbyes, had already embarrassed himself with Adams, had no desire to do so again.

Michael walked with Adams through the gate to the front.

"Andrew Giles. He was one of them, who used the service provided by the bastard. That's why we were able to make use of him, he was terrified he would be found out." As the taxi pulled up they shook hands. Michael pulled Adams towards him and hugged. He wasn't expecting that.

"I wouldn't give evidence against the creep in a court of law but you may be able to use the information. Besides, he'll get caught he's becoming careless. Saturday nights, Kings Cross, he likes a bit of rough."

*****

The 'bollocking' he received from Detective Chief Superintendent Arthur Fisher was not as bad as he thought it would be. This was due in part to the intelligence he was able to pass on to the Paedophile Unit.

The winding up of the investigation in all took another ten weeks. It still needed to go to trial but given the fact Albie Tate was detained in a secure hospital and they had his taped confession, there would be little media interest.

During this time Adams was confined to clearing up paperwork on this and other cases.

It had been decided not to continue with the Monique Cecile investigation until interest in the William Smith case had died down. Besides as Jimmy Benton pointed out to all concerned forensics needed at least six weeks to work on the trace evidence.

Speculation about Jake Mortimer died down after a couple of weeks. Adams let it be known that Jake had decided to stay on in France to help his family with the renovations of the chateau. The general consensus was 'lucky beggar'.

Freddie Smith, well he wasn't going anywhere. His parole had been granted on condition he lived at the halfway house. He felt safe on his home patch, he would slip up and Adams would be there when he did. Adams was convinced that Freddie murdered George Parker, he just needed the evidence, but he was a patient man. He kept in contact with Detective Inspector Dave Spencer of Kent Police.

The investigating team had been disbanded. Adams asked to keep a minimum of six officers ready for when they could pursue the Monique Cecile case in earnest. Arthur Fisher said he was in no position to make demands, would be lucky to keep the case. Fisher gave him Jimmy Benton and Gill Cole. Julie Burton if her uniformed supervisor was prepared to allow her secondment to his team.

Chapter 41

Adams and Jimmy Benton had arranged to meet Dave Spencer in The Admiral Nelson, Blue Town. Officially, they were visiting Harty Churchyard where Monique Cecile's remains had been found. Unofficially they had been assisting him with the George Parker murder investigation.

"Saw you on the box last night. Glad you took my advice and wore a dark suit." Dave Spencer smiled, put the two pints of beer on the table.

"Did the appeal throw up anything interesting?"

A woman rang in. She remembered George Parker from way back. He had been working on the island during the summer of seventy-two. She was only thirteen at the time but he plied her with drink and had sex with her. She didn't have any relevant information, just wanted to let us know she was glad the bastard had copped it. It confirmed Jimmy Benton's suspicions that both Parker and William Smith were active on the island in the late sixties and early seventies.

Adams told him about Freddie Smith. Freddie had slipped out of the prison on a shopping trip. Adams' guess would be drugs for the Driscoll cousins. Dave Spencer had to agree his intelligence was that the Driscolls ran that side of the business within the prison complex on the Isle of Sheppey. The knife he would have hidden nearby. Dave told him a search of the area revealed no weapon; they had assumed it had been thrown into the sea.

"The time of the Monique Cecile murder, did you log any calls regarding 'suspect goings on' around Harty Church? It's pretty isolated and clannish. Strangers would have been noticed." Dave Spencer shook his head. He had got one of his clerks to look back in the records but she didn't turn anything up. A more detailed investigation would require authority from Adams' boss to the head of Kent C.I.D. Given Adams' standing at the moment, it would be near impossible for such a request to be granted.

Adams had already spoken to the relatives of the deceased whose grave had been violated. The daughter remembered the sequence of events vividly, still missed her mother even after all these years. She had been to the church the day before the funeral to check on the arrangements. She met one of the Church Wardens there. As there was no electricity in the church he opened the outside security shutters so she was able to arrange flowers in there as a celebration of her mother's life. The newly dug grave had been ready but she had no desire to go over to it.

The Church Warden who was filling up the oil lamps ready for the following day also when interviewed could remember nothing of significance. Now in his eighties his memory wasn't what it used to be.

The one thing he did recall however was the tyre tracks. The grounds of the churchyard had been an obsession with him at that time. There were tyre tracks over the grass verge but he assumed they were from the van the workmen used to haul their equipment. He remembered the tracks as he had already complained to the council about the van and thought the driver had driven on the verge deliberately.

Adams also told Dave Spencer about the young boy abducted by William Smith. When the investigation had been completed, Kent Police would get a full report from their Paedophile Unit. Dave Spencer was grateful for the help. The boy was one of the outstanding cases he inherited when he became an inspector.

Adams' mobile went off. A number of the local drinkers glared and one pointed to a sign above the bar. He excused himself and walked outside to take the call, it was Paula Rogers, graduate in criminal psychology who was working for him. She was desperate to join the force as a lowly plod, work her way up the ranks. Adams had promised to see what he could do. She was so excited, he had to tell her to calm down and speak more slowly.

"Well sir, I assumed that our body was put into the grave the evening she was due in on the ferry and checked out traffic tickets on the most obvious route to the island. I then cross referenced the names against police and court personnel for the time you thought William Smith had seen the killer." Adams was seriously impressed. A name had jumped out at her.

"We should be back just after lunch, see you then." Ever since Freddie had told them that the killer was part of the judiciary system he had been careful to ensure only those involved in the case were informed of developments.

They stopped off at Clacketts Lane Services for a quick sandwich. Adams told Jimmy of his conversation with Paula.

"Bright one that. Make a good detective." Adams had to agree. Unfortunately, her uncle, the Chief Constable had other plans for his intelligent niece.

Adams walked into the incident room bearing gifts of seaside rock. Jimmy Benton followed with pizza and fizzy drinks.

"You do know how to give a girl a good time," Julie teased.

"Right what have we got?"

"Not what sir, who!"

Andrew Giles had been given a ticket on the A2 between Faversham and Sittingbourne very late that night. Jimmy Benton checked the passenger list from the ferry. Andrew Giles had not been listed.

"Shall we bring him in Guv?"

"Not yet. We need to be really sure he's involved." Adams wanted to check Andrew Giles out in greater detail. Around the time of the murder he would have been about nineteen years old. From what Michael Smith had told them Andrew Giles was more interested in young boys. He asked Jimmy Benton to check into Andrew Giles' background, which university he attended, when he began practising law, who his friends were. He knew that Jimmy would be discreet.

After the briefing was over, Adams went into a private office; he called a number he never expected to use again.

"I need to speak with you. No not there, somewhere we

won't be recognised." They agreed a place and he put the 'phone down without saying goodbye. It had been almost four months, he wondered if she had changed much.

It took him some time to find the restaurant. It was off the beaten track. She hadn't changed, still looked as beautiful and classy as he remembered. He leaned across and kissed her gently. She turned her head at the moment he expected to taste her lips.

"I didn't think I would ever hear from you again." She spoke in a formal voice as though she was giving evidence in the dock.

"How's the family?"

"We're doing fine. Jean and Shirley have come into the business with me. Jake well he's still in France with Michael. They've set up a bed and breakfast business in the chateau. Michael and I share the cost of Mary in a private hospital. Say what you came to say and then we need never meet again." Adams was hoping they could have a civilised meal together but Christine hadn't even bothered to remove her coat.

"Andrew Giles. Do you see him socially? How long has he been your solicitor?"

"Not long. His father looked after my affairs. When Herbert Giles passed away Andrew took over the business. He had been working as an associate and just took over his father's clients. As for whether I see him socially well that really is none of your business." Adams picked up the menu, asked her what she fancied.

"I fancied you."

Chapter 42

Adams and Jimmy Benton carried out the background checks on Andrew Giles. Jimmy was curious as to why Jake had disappeared from the scene but he kept his own counsel. Adams would tell him in his own time.

He was anxious not to involve any of the serving officers in this task. Should Andrew Giles get to hear what was going on it could blow up in their faces. He wanted to keep the fall out to a minimum. Besides Andrew Giles was a Mason in the same Lodge as a number of serving officers, Bryan Low included.

Not a great lover of the Internet, Adams was amazed at the amount of information you could find on an individual if you knew where to look and young Paula certainly did. He hadn't wanted to get her involved but as she so rightly pointed out, they couldn't suspend her, she wasn't one of them anyway, just a humble research student. She detailed to him her findings.

In 1966 Andrew Giles was in his final year at Southampton University studying law. According to the results he didn't do particularly well, just scraped a lowly degree. From the university archives she was able to find out he was secretary of the Young Conservatives and a leading light in the Amateur Dramatic Society.

From the company website, they were able to find out what he did with his spare time now. Apparently, many of his summers were spent assisting with a holiday club run by his Baptist Church. His father encouraged him to immerse himself in the local community.

"Impressionable deprived kids. I wonder if he took them camping in Kent? Under canvas, ideal place for him to groom his victims."

As instructed, Adams had kept his distance from Freddie Smith. Uniform had been keeping tabs on his behalf. Told him about Freddie's move from the Halfway House to a flat nearby. But with the William Smith case now with the DPP, there was no reason he couldn't lean on him. Freddie would have begun to be complacent not expecting a visit.

Freddie was living in private rented accommodation on the Abelard Estate. According to the last report from his Parole Officer, Freddie was an example to her other clients, working part time for the corporation and keeping out of trouble.

Adams took Gill Cole with him to the interview. A perceptive officer, he valued her opinion.

"Anything I should know in particular about Freddie Smith Guv?"

"He has issues with women. Thinks they're all stupid and only useful for one thing."

"So you want me to take the lead in the interview then?"

"Exactly."

Freddie had just woken. In fact their insistent knocking had forced him out of bed. He was not best pleased when he opened the door.

"Unsociable hour, might have known it would be the filth."

"Mr Smith?" Gill Cole showed him her warrant card. Adams stood behind, not bothering with his.

"Sorry love you're not my type." Freddie went to shut the door but Gill Cole was quicker.

"Thanks for inviting us in." He shrugged and wandered into the kitchen.

"That's kind of you sir, coffee no sugar. We'll wait in the lounge." Before he had time to reply Gill and Jonathan Adams had made themselves comfortable on a leather settee.

"Sorry love I'm all out of drinks."

"Nice furniture Mr Smith, the corporation must be paying you well, or did you find this on the dump?" Now he was really annoyed.

Adams decided it was time to intervene. Told Freddie either they talked here or they could take him out in handcuffs and speak formally at the station.

"What do you want to know?"

He asked Freddie if he could recall any more conversations with his father about the death of Monique Cecile.

"Such as?"

"The name of the killer would be useful."

"All I know is that he is an important person in the police. The old man said he would pay plenty to keep his secret."

"Did your father receive the money as cash or was it deposited into a bank account?" Freddie looked up.

"She talking to me?" Gill Cole smiled at Freddie, then without warning stuck her face directly in front of his.

"Listen you 'arsehole', a word in the right ear and you will be investigated for downloading child pornography. Maybe kept overnight in the cells. 'Ponces' aren't segregated in our little nick."

"I don't do kids."

"Probably not but once the idea is out there, well who knows!" Adams was impressed.

These last few months Freddie Smith had been cultivating an image of a villain on the up. Even hardened criminals had no time for paedophiles. His business would be hard hit. Any hint he was a child molester, well.

"You've taught the bitch well, she's more of a bastard than you are." Gill Cole thanked him for the compliment.

"The money was always in cash. It was left at a post office box. Both him and the old man had a key." Freddie had on occasions accompanied his old man when he collected the money. Once, he staked out the post office to catch the killer, get the money for himself but nothing came of it. As they left, Gill stopped at the end of the landing and shouted back.

"Thanks for you help Mr Smith we'll be in touch." Adams shook his head.

"That'll get the neighbours talking." She was still wound up when they got back to the car.

"Can you believe it? The killer is using the post office

opposite the nick to make his drop!" Adams said he could. The killer was one of their own; it would be convenient for him to do so. Gill Cole looked at him waiting for him to elaborate.

As they drove back Adams recounted his previous conversations with Freddie Smith. Gill was pleased that she had been taken into his confidence.

"Who else knows?"

"Just the boss and a select few."

"Any idea who?"

"Male between the ages of thirty seven to sixty. Jimmy Benton and Paula are cross referencing passenger lists with personnel."

"Well we could narrow it down a little more. The killer was left handed according to the pathologists report. The angle of the blow, he had to be at least six inches taller than Monique. She was five foot five, so we are looking at a six feet plus left handed male. What else do we know?"

"Well Andrew Giles was caught speeding in the area on the same evening the ferry docked. But he has a watertight alibi, was attending some charity function, with a number of police officers as witnesses."

"So it's someone with a connection to our learned friend. Why haven't we brought him in for questioning yet?"

"If I bring him in too early, he could warn the killer. I need to have a good idea of the killer's identity before I confront Mr Andrew Giles. Besides, I'm not sure we have enough evidence yet to get him for accessory after the fact."

Chapter 43

Adams glanced at the caller identification on his mobile phone. It took a moment before he realised who it was. He hesitated before answering.

"I thought I told you to forget this number!" The caller uncertain if he should speak.

"I know but this is important to the case you must be working on. Not over the 'phone though. I'm not sure who can be trusted there."

The original agreement was Jake Mortimer would not contact him again. It was a shame but it would keep them both safe that way. Jake however was making a visit to the UK, had important new information on the Monique Cecile case. The meet was to be at Clacketts Lane services. Jake was already there when he arrived.

He told him about their chateau being only five kilometres from the Cecile family home. The copper in him just couldn't resist it. He looked up the local archived news on her disappearance and made a few enquiries in the village. It seemed the summer prior to her travelling to the UK, Monique and a few girlfriends took up with a group of English students grape picking in the area. Veronique, one of the friends now married to the local mayor, invited them to a meal at her home.

They enjoyed welcoming visitors to their pretty village as it gave them the chance to brush up on their English. Claude took Michael to sample the delights of his wine cellar, leaving him to speak to Veronique. She told him about her special friend. Monique had been a beauty, all the young men wanted to go out with her. She was unaware of her effect on the English students. She showed Jake the only photograph she had to remember her friend by. She kindly allowed him to make a copy.

"Thought it might help." He handed it over to Adams.

"I've scribbled on the back some of the names that

Veronique could recall.

"Thanks. How long are you staying?"

"I've a ferry to catch this evening." They shook hands. Jake gave him a business card for the bed and breakfast.

"Visit any time."

Adams purchased another cup of coffee and studied the photograph. It was of a group of young people, sitting by a river. In the middle of the group was Monique Cecile but it was the young man standing on the edge of the group who interested him. The face looked familiar; there was no mistaking the teenage youth. He shook his head in disbelief.

"Governor, it's me. I need to see you regarding the Monique Cecile investigation. We may have a problem."

*****

Julie checked the personal effects' log. No keys were listed. Armed with a photograph of the deceased she walked to the post office.

She struck lucky with cashier number twelve. Her seat was next to the entrance door to the boxes. She remembered William Smith. On occasions, he would arrive drunk; struggle with his swipe card and cause a scene. A member of staff would go out and release the door for him. The cashier's friendly chat was interrupted by a voice directly behind her.

"Constable Burton, I do hope you're not here on personal business." Startled, Julie turned, stared at the person who had tapped her on the shoulder. Trying not to appear too surprised, she hastily regained her composure.

"No sir, we need a letter sent recorded. Sergeant Dexter sent me over." He smiled and leaned across to use his swipe card. She thanked the cashier for all her help and rushed back to the office.

Inspector Bryan Low. Julie knew he and Adams didn't get on and Bryan Low wasn't well liked, but he had a certain charm with the female officers, was good looking but boy did he know it.

*****

"Have you any evidence apart from a black and white photo and the word of this French woman?"

"No but I will get it. Now I know where to go looking."

"All this photo proves is that he may have known Monique Cecile."

"So why never mention it to any of us? I need to find the link between him and Andrew Giles, I aim to take them both down for the murder."

"This is to be kept strictly between us for the time being. There could be a perfectly innocent reason for him not mentioning it. Any spurious rumours could ruin his career. He could sue and then my career could be ruined."

Adams handed over the brown envelope, the photograph locked securely in the Superintendent's office. Fortunately he had made a copy on the way in.

Julie could hardly contain her excitement when she arrived back at the incident room. She recounted to Adams her visit to the post office.

"Lots of coppers use the boxes but it wouldn't hurt to make a few discreet enquiries." He told Julie to forget what she had seen for the time being, it could jeopardise his enquiries if it became public knowledge.

Adams needed to find a connection between Andrew Giles and his suspect, he knew just who to ask. Sitting in the canteen chatting to Duty Sergeant Dexter, he brought up the subject of Andrew Giles. How come he was on such personal terms with certain police officers?

"The Lodge, they are all probably in the same lodge."

"You in the lodge too Dex?"

"Nope but sometimes Inspector high and mighty Low drops a pile of letters at the front desk, says to put them with our post. Lodge business, funny business if you ask me." Adams nodded to James Macdonald as he advanced towards him with his dinner tray.

"His profession, he's probably one of them too."

Ignoring them both James Macdonald sat down at an empty table. He still had not forgiven Adams for the perceived slight on his integrity and professionalism.

To carry out the autopsy on the remains of Monique Cecile should have been his task. Using the Forensic Science Services gave out the message that he wasn't up to it. Adams was in two minds whether to offer an olive branch to the pathologist but decided he was more likely to ram it down this throat.

Adams had to leave investigating the personnel records to the boss. Arthur Fisher had the clearance needed. Lowly detective sergeants like Adams were only good for investigating the likes of Freddie Smith, which was exactly what he, intended to do.

"Tell me Julie why do you drive like a boy racer?"

"Lots of brothers sir, anyway it's a gift I have." Adams felt sure it was more a curse.

Julie beamed at Freddie as he opened the front door. He scowled at Adams.

"See you left the Rottweiller at home this time."

"He's brought the pussycat with him today but remember cats have claws."

"People will start to talk, you keep coming round. Your other mate turned you then?" Adams walked into the kitchen and began opening cupboards and drawers. "Where is it then?"

"What?"

"The key. Personal effects went to next of kin, you!"

"No idea what you are talking about and I'll have you if you've not got a warrant."

"Just looking for the tea or coffee."

"Sir, can I be the arresting officer?" They both turned to stare at Julie Burton.

"Arrested for what?"

"Accessory to murder, withholding vital evidence. Crime against fashion with that shirt." Adams suppressed a laugh; he had to agree the shirt was dreadful.

"You'll not get any more money out of him. We're closing in. If you don't hand over the key, I'll assume you are in on it. She wasn't much more than a child. You know what they do to child killers inside." The tone of his voice, Freddie realised he was deadly serious.

He reached into the cupboard under the sink. Taped behind the waste pipe was the key. Freddie pealed off the tape and threw the key on the floor. Julie picked it up and thanked him for his co-operation, told him she was still in two minds about arresting him over the shirt though. Adams declined the offer of a drink, had things to do, people to arrest.

On the way back he arranged for Scenes of Crime to meet Julie at the post office.

"Any fingerprints on the inside of the box. The report is to come direct to me!"

Chapter 44

As a personal favour to Adams the Senior Scenes of Crime Officer took charge of the task. The box was dusted inside and out and on the top. He had already been supplied with prints from William and Freddie Smith for elimination.

The tests finished he called Adams. All prints except for two had been eliminated. Adams went across to speak with him.

"Can you run the print through staff personnel records for me."

"Is there something I should know about?"

"This is higher up the food chain than you or I. Whatever is found, the information must stay between us for the time being!" He said he understood, asked which personnel department he should start with. Adams requested he contact him when he had the information.

He drove to Jimmy Benton's house. The message on his voicemail sounded urgent. Jimmy had found out something very interesting about Mr Andrew Giles whilst he was a university student. He declined a beer, Jimmy shrugged he wasn't driving or on the force anymore, could have a drink whenever he wanted. He had printed out the information. Adams flicked through the pages as he walked back to his car. Armed with the last piece of the puzzle everything was in place, all he needed to do now was to speak to Arthur Fisher.

He was to go to the boss's home, too many Masons and careless talk at the station. Adams had never been there before. It was out in the sticks, took him a while to find it. Mrs Fisher, a small slight woman in her early sixties opened the door, she showed him into her husband's den.

They discussed if it was time to bring in Andrew Giles. Adams told him about Giles changing faculties after his first year at university. That was the connection between him and the killer. Fisher told him the decision had been made to bring them both in on Monday morning. He was applying for the warrants through a magistrate who was most definitely not a Mason and who knew neither man socially.

Fisher also wanted Freddie Smith out of the way. Adams said he would arrange for Dave Spencer of the Kent Police to request Freddie's help with his enquiries into the murder of George Parker.

Jimmy and Adams again met Dave Spencer in the Admiral Nelson, Blue Town on the Isle of Sheppey.

"People are beginning to think you're two of my regulars. Can't you find another pub? Coppers are bad for business." They sat at their usual corner table.

"Have we got any further information to justify them taking him in?" Adams nodded.

Freddie Smith would be taken into custody early Monday morning and driven straight to Sittingbourne Police Station for questioning. He passed over to the Kent detective the new intelligence he had on the murder.

"Still not enough to charge him with."

"Just keep him as long as you can."

*****

Andrew Giles had not been expecting visitors so early in the morning, was not prepared to let them in. Gill Cole produced the warrant for his arrest and pushed her way inside the house. A noise caused the two uniformed officers attending to sprint upstairs.

The two underage boys who had been sharing his bed were brought into the drawing room. Andrew Giles told them to say nothing. They were allowed to dress while Gill Cole radioed for a representative from Social Services to take them into care. She checked her watch. Both arrests were to be made at the same time. She was curious as to who the other person would be.

Officers outside the area assisted Detective Superintendent Arthur Fisher and Detective Sergeant Jonathan Adams to make their arrest.

He didn't come quietly. Told them they had no idea who they were dealing with. They would both be out of a job by the end of the day. He was taken for interview to a nick outside their division. Once there, he refused to speak, not even to ask for a solicitor.

The Chief Super spoke at length with the Custody Sergeant. They were to be informed if he requested a solicitor and under no circumstances were his whereabouts to be disclosed to staff from their nick as there may be others implicated.

"Understood sir."

"He can sweat for a few hours. We've a solicitor to interview."

It was agreed that Arthur Fisher would interview Andrew Giles. Adams would be the assisting officer. Gill Cole took Adams to one side.

"Caught with underage boys Guv. He should be co-operative." Adams smiled at Gill Cole.

Andrew Giles turned out not to be as co-operative as they imagined. He refused to answer any questions until his solicitor arrived.

"That's fine Mr Giles, we want to talk to you about another incident. Accessory to the murder of Monique Cecile on the 30th July 1966." He looked directly at Jonathan Adams.

"Now I know you've really lost it!"

"Cast your mind back to the evening of Saturday the 30th. We'd just won the World Cup. Do you remember where you were? Me, I was patrolling the town centre of Brighton, keeping German students away from the English fans. Detective Sergeant Adams, well I would imagine he was trying to get himself a girlfriend."

Gill Cole entered the interview room. Adams announced the time, her name and rank. He quickly read the note she gave him and passed it on to Arthur Fisher.

"Detective Sergeant Adams is leaving the room and Detective Sergeant Cole will remain."

Out in reception Adams shook hand with Andrew Giles' solicitor. Peregrine Jones a Senior Partner at Levy Jones & Associates. Adams took him into a small interview room to outline the charges against his client.

"I've no idea why he contacted our office. We've had nothing to do with him!"

"That's the reason Perry. He wants to keep it away from his own business contacts."

"I'm not sure I want him as a client! What do you want me to do?" Adams outlined his proposal.

A half hour break to allow Giles to confer with his solicitor was arranged.

Adams made a quick call to the Custody Sergeant of the other station. He confirmed that there had been no calls concerning the prisoner. He had taken charge of him personally. As regulations required, he had again formally asked if he wanted a solicitor. He had again said no.

Gill Cole approached Adams.

"Guv, we're not going to do a deal are we? Men like him think they can just buy whatever they want. Those kids, someone needs to stand up for them." Adams assured her they had no intention of letting him get away with the indecent assault of the boys. Even though they were not prepared to talk, there was enough physical evidence to convict him.

They reconvened the interview after a hurried lunch.

Andrew Giles sat passively in the chair, letting Perry Jones do his talking.

"I have spoken at length with my client. He will admit to offering a lift to a stranded hitchhiker on the 30th May 1966. At the time, he had no idea they would meet again. Indeed, he didn't even remember the encounter, had to be reminded when they met quite by chance at the Sessions Court."

Fisher produced documentary evidence that far from being strangers they had in fact both attended Southampton University at the same time.

"My client studied law. The faculties were in different

buildings, in different parts of the town. They never mixed.

"Did he know about your interest in young boys? Catch you bringing them back to the room you shared?" Perry looked at his client and shook his head.

"Did he not tell you? Andrew here dropped out of his original course, couldn't make the grade. Ended up doing law. Still I expect your father was pleased at your change of heart." Perry asked to confer with his client again. The tape recorders were stopped and Fisher and Adams went out to stretch their legs.

"Perry's not happy about representing him. If he doesn't start telling the truth, he'll be without a solicitor!" Within minutes they were called back in.

"My client admits to collecting his friend. But categorically denies knowing anything about the murder of Monique Cecile. He was woken by a telephone call very late that night. His friend was in a bit of a state. He said that his car had been stolen, he was stranded and needed a lift home."

"For the tape Mr Giles, please state the name of your friend." Andrew Giles mumbled.

"For the sake of the tape. Please speak clearly."

"Macdonald, James Macdonald."

Chapter 45

Once he started, all the hate and fear he felt for James Macdonald came pouring out. At times crying and snivelling like a small child, he made Adams' skin crawl. He couldn't help it. Children they are so much kinder you see. He related to them much better than he could with adults. Sharply, Adams told him to stick to the facts concerning James Macdonald.

James had been the best student on the course. He would ridicule his attempts at his course work, belittle him at every opportunity. Thanks to James Macdonald, he had a breakdown and had to leave. All he had ever wanted was to be a doctor. His father managed to get him on to a law course but his nerves were so bad, he only just scraped a degree.

"I was still frightened of him so when he rang that night for a lift, I was unable to say no."

"Nothing to do with the incident of the young boy in the room you shared with James Macdonald then?" Andrew Giles coloured.

"I think you must have been mistaken."

By the time Andrew Giles had finished pouring out his life story Adams and Fisher felt they had enough to confront James Macdonald.

*****

The Custody Sergeant confirmed that the prisoner had made no calls even though he had been offered the opportunity and was still declining the offer of a solicitor.

"Best get on with it then."

James Macdonald had lost none of his arrogance. The mask slipped only when Adams requested a DNA sample. Adams pointed out to him that he had no choice seeing as he was being charged with murder and anyway, if he was as innocent as he claimed, then he could be easily eliminated from their enquiries.

James Macdonald again refused the offer of a solicitor. Adamantly informing them he would be representing himself in court, Arthur Fisher strongly counselled him against the idea.

They questioned him about his association with Andrew Giles. He told them he didn't associate with perverts. Why then did he request a lift from him on the night of the murder of Monique Cecile? He denied having done so. James Macdonald knew that it would be his word against that of Andrew Giles and was confident they would believe him.

"Are you telling us that you never met Monique Cecile?"

"She was taken to Birmingham before we were able to be introduced." He laughed as his own joke.

They asked him about the summer of 1966. Where was he living? Was he still at university? Did he work during the summer?

"I should imagine I was in digs in Southampton and I certainly can't recall if I had a summer job!" Adams offered to jog his memory. Provided documentation that during the summer of 1965, along with a group of other students he worked in the Provence region of France. The student union had arranged block insurance for the duration of their stay. He was shown the photograph of the group and was asked to confirm that he was in the group. He shrugged, said it looked like him, but he couldn't recall that long ago. Fortunately Arthur Fisher told him Southampton University could.

They then went on to interrogate him about the events leading up to the murder. Asked him why he didn't return to the grape picking the next year.

"How can I answer that question, when I am unable to recall that I did grape picking the year before?"

"No matter, we can help you there. The summer of 1966 you worked temporarily as a cleaner on one of the cross channel ferries."

"If you say so."

"Not just me but the personnel records of the shipping company."

It had taken some time but Paula had the idea if he wasn't a passenger then perhaps he was a member of the crew.

"I don't recall."

"Is that why you are such a lousy pathologist, you have difficulty in recalling things?" He took them both by surprise, jumping up and attempting to overturn the table.

"I'm a brilliant pathologist, you have no idea!"

"Not as good at those working for the Forensic Science Service though!" Adams' retort stopped him in his tracks. Now he looked confused, unsure of himself.

Arthur Fisher decided it would be the ideal time to take a break.

"That put the wind up him!" He looked across at his Detective Sergeant.

"Have we a breakthrough with the forensics?"

"No idea but it has got him worried." Adams' contact at the forensic laboratory had advised him it would be at least a few more hours before they completed all the tests. He had promised to contact Adams immediately the results were available.

"So Jonathan do you think we've got enough to convict?"

"We will have sir. He's a dangerous man. If he had gotten wind of what was happening he would have been out of the country by now. We needed to take him in when we did."

During the break Adams contacted Jimmy Benton. Word of the arrest had leaked out. They were fending off calls from the local and national press. They even had an outside broadcast van from the local television news parked outside the building.

He told Adams that Andrew Giles had crumbled. His solicitor was going for the stress and illness plea. Adams asked if Gill had managed to get any more information from

Andrew Giles on James Macdonald.

"Only that he was a very predatory individual. Arrogant in the extreme."

They were unable to continue with the interrogation as James Macdonald decided he would like legal representation after all.

"He's worried we have forensics to tie him in."

An hour later Adams received the call he had been waiting for.

Forensics is exactly what they had. A microscopic droplet of dried blood was discovered on the inside lining of one of Monique Cecile's boots. Blood from the deep scratch she had inflicted under James Macdonald's eye as she fought for her life.

Detective Sergeant Jonathan Adams formally arrested Dr James Macdonald for the murder of Monique Cecile. An application for bail was refused. He would be remanded to Pentonville Prison to await trial.

Despite a 'not guilty' plea and a vigorous defence argument James Macdonald was found guilty and sentenced to life imprisonment. Madam Cecile lived just long enough to see justice done for her daughter.

The Paedophile Unit uncovered evidence that Andrew Giles was an active member of the same extensive network as William Smith and George Parker. This made the deal his solicitors had thrashed out with Arthur Fisher null and void. Adams made sure that Inspector Dave Spencer of the Kent Police received recognition for his assistance in the case.

No arrests were made for the murder of George Parker, despite the best efforts of Jonathan Adams, Kent Police and Crimewatch UK.

But Adams was a patient man, would bide his time.